d● t

Mara Anne McQuire

ISBN: 979-8-9958988-0-1

DEDICATION

For the 1.6 percent

CONTENTS

Chapter *Page*

The line, the words, the… fucking contronym… 1

it's usually only a handful of men who get to decide to go fuck with someone, war chooses you. 22

Muhbee iz uh tess. 42

The fourth is time. 53

Ten minutes of that will get you back into the right side of your day. 100

… too heinous to be tried by only one state. 121

Something tells me this book has never been its cover. 131

I was going to say spooky, but you'd redline the hell out of that. 142

Any day that starts with a little bump and ends with Narcan is never a good day… 152

These are second date questions, or if you're really cute, 3rd martini at the very least. 121

We can't be seen throwing the FBI under the bus. They do a pretty good job of that by themselves -- they don't need our help. 163

Spoof positive. 169

ACKNOWLEDGMENTS

Unlike dot, no woman is an island (which would be dreadful indeed if we were) and I prefer to think of us as a Galaxy, pun intended, which by the time you're finished reading this story, will seem "on brand" as the kids would say. Here the flowers of gratitude and appreciation go to my dear sisters who read first drafts (which nobody should have to endure) and encouraged me to soldier on and my new favorite publishing family, the gang of story nerds and rebel writers at ZBP, who believed in an unsigned writer and her disaster of a first, second and third drafts then kicked my butt literally across the finish line. They believed in me more than I ever did myself. May you too have a Zuzubean Press in your life.

And no. I am no hostage and write this of my free will.

Seriously.

Really.

No, really

1

"

The line, the words, the… fucking contronym…

"

"I didn't start out this way?... Okay, by now, we all know that's bullshit."

"She watched from plainsight. It had to be plainsight. That was the way. She had many self-invented words to describe her actions and techniques. It was to instill she said, 'a handrail for discipline.' It was as if she was reading aloud from a handbook or a manual.

I would come to find out, she *was*, one that she had written herself. Or, more accurately, was writing in present tense. By now, according to my editor, you're looking for the name of the woman I'm describing, since I'm using feminine pronouns.

The name is easy. She is Illinois State inmate number W10042574, but her friends (and soon the media, including this magazine) may refer to her simply, as dot. Not Dot as in, short for Dorothy, 'dot' as in the character between two named pieces of data, like dot com. But, and here's the thing, I started calling her that *after* I… okay, started to *connect the dots* with the calling card left behind at each of her now confessed and verified murder scenes. A vital piece of evidence that the FBI hadn't ever released. Nor, will they, I'm guessing, before the posting of this.

You're also probably hoping for a description.

I've yet to see her fully. I've caught glimpses of a single eye close enough to the grimy and scratched, postcard-sized window in her cell door, to tell its color: hazel. I had thought them blue for the longest time until they were green one day.

Of course, her head has been shaved by her warders, not a standard practice for a person who just walks in one day and turns herself in, but then, rarely has someone confessed to a string of murders spanning seven states, that is, if all of her facts check out. I have caught brief glimpses when she's turned her head and what I've seen shows a gentle graying in dark… red… red-*ish* or maybe once was *red?* stubble.

Her mind is very sharp and I found our sanctioned conversations over what has been the agreed two-week period as she awaits arraignment, both, fascinating and oddly illuminating. Her motives are very clear. Her remorse is non-existent. Her confidence in her actions are not the justifications of a radicalized zealot, but more like the calm observations of a witness, a scientist, an analyst, and are just as unshakable. As if she has the benefit of oversight. An aerial view of all sides of an issue and its past, present, and future implications."

"Bitch, please. You're not seriously considering publishing that?"

Meghan stopped her recording. "What?"

dot's eye pressed up to the glass. This was how she froze time for Meghan. Figuratively holding her aloft by the scruff of her neck, like a mama cat, gently discipling her kitten. Meghan would try to breathe through the sudden weightlessness, the sudden disorientation, more worried that at any time dot would end the interview, cut off her access, and there would go her story.

dot's eye stared unblinking, today it was a light gray, as if all color had been drained from it. In truth, it merely reflected the gray walls and gray sky through the only window in the entire cell suite, which was as Meghan had been told, reserved for high-profile cases. The thin sliver of a window in the "observation area" just outside dot's actual cell, revealed a late spring gloom hung over the Stateville State Prison, or 'The Pen,' as it was fondly referred, just outside Chicago's western plain.

dot's gaze softened. She blinked once as if to release Meghan and receded into the dim of the cell. Meghan tried to shrug off the stare, tried to remember where she was. Her handwritten notes, still in her hands. She slumped down onto the bench, rereading to see what had drawn the question.

Meghan Woods was late thirties, Black. Her button-down shirttails, pale triangles on the thighs of her black cotton jeans peaked out from under a Peacoat.

Meghan took her first breath in all this time, "Well, yes. This is serious, therefore, I am ser…"

"Come on, Meghan…Oversight?"

"It's a metaphor."

"It's inaccurate."

"It's… inaccurate?"

"And it's a double entendre. And not in a good way, making it a contranym."

Meghan stared at her notes.

The eye appeared at the glass. Was she gloating? Looking for acknowledgment? Observing?

The line, the words, the… *fucking contronym*… Meghan's arms slumped to her sides. She felt the eye and grudgingly made contact. dot's eye winked, "Careful, your editors will claim you've gone native. And for the record, I would ordinarily rock that one, but, it's important you get this right. For your sake. As for the rest of it… past, present, sure… it's a bit boastful, but it's not like they didn't have it coming.

But future? It hasn't occurred yet… and everyone's gonna wanna know how you know what I see? And if I did have oversight of the future, would I have seen this? Or are you throwing shade, in which case, I would salute you. It's bold, but still not accurate. So I would salute your boldness, but not your accuracy."

Meghan shook her head. "You are fucking exhausting." She slashed the line from her notes. "Anything else?

The eye receded again. "That's enough for today."

Meghan opened her mouth to protest but felt the fatigue in her shoulders. Maybe dot was right? "I've only got a week left with you. They don't count the weekend, so that's only five days."

Meghan could hear the gentle complaint of the bedsprings from deep in dot's cell, "We'll get it all. Scout's honor."

Meghan stood and walked to the door, she raised her hand to knock but the electric growl of the steel door announced its opening before her knuckles could touch. The door slid open and the rush of danker and colder air jostled in beside her. She looked around for hidden cameras, found none, glanced over her shoulder in dot's direction, and then stepped out onto the catwalk-like balcony of the prison. "Be careful out there," yelled dot from behind her as the growl announced the door's closing and then, Meghan was alone on the iron and concrete as the steel door's slamming echoed above all.

"Fuck." She whispered under her breath and made her way to the exit.

"Fuck."

*****

Meghan had taken the EL as far as it went that morning then transferred to a hire car. The mag was picking up her expenses, but she needed the extra money (whatever the amount) to make it through; there was always so much month left at the end of the money, as her mother would say. She'd put in for mileage rather than reimbursement. It was a lower amount, (big surprise there) calculated at pre-pandemic rates, which always made her grind her teeth, but then, in today's world, what didn't? But at least she wouldn't have to save her receipts.

Now she was reversing the transportation process. And almost home.

Of all her recent assignments, this was the one she had actually pushed for. And until dot had turned herself in, no one had known just how qualified Meghan would turn out to be. Was it chance or by design? And answer which would depend on who was asked. Meghan would credit it to kismet, or as her Auntie would say bashert, but dot would say design.

That is, of course… hers. And she would also, of course, be right.

Shit started to get real, as Meghan would say when she was found her way to the actual crime scene. (it was a national murder spree at this point, though nobody who should be able to do anything about had figured that pout yet stretching from Oregon to Connecticut and as far south as Alabama & Florida). Meghan had found herself in a strange ad-hoc… well, some might say *cult*. This motley band of professional reporters seemed to sense the connections when even the local jurisdictions did not. They started on a true-crime Substack, then moved to Signal to trade tips from their police and sheriff contacts, theories and even gossip as they followed a macabre trail of breadcrumbs, bonded in their search, camaraderie and bewilderment that the authorities didn't or maybe wouldn't see what they saw…

Each murder was different. Specific. Almost unrelated. Except for the dots. All were not equally brutal, but, all were equally… *meaningful?* Or rather full of meaning, a constant debate among her fellow reporters in the cult. Meghan had used effective, which hadn't caught on among her colleagues, but that didn't stop her.

Meaning-full.

And oddly, it hadn't been the dots that had led her to here. Those, the dots, were still a mystery to be solved. A single sheet of printing paper, innocuous, as though it had been taken almost as an afterthought from the household's seldom-used printer on the way out the door. But… it was never from the same ream and it was never the same pen. It was a simple drawing; three dots connected by a single line. Never the same pattern, either. Leading the police, the FBI, and (though the FBI would never admit it) Interpol to surmise each murder had a different suspect.

The working theory was a cell, though the ideology had yet to be discovered.

And of course no fingerprints. No connection to the store where the paper had been bought, nor the lot number or the manufacturer who made it. Same with the pens. Usually, there's a subtle chemical signature which can be traced to its plant. Except, no.

The dots and their maker had been invisible until they were visible, like Schrödinger's cat.

Which was a name considered to label the string of murders, but (luckily?) deemed too esoteric for today's readers.

Like.

As.

As if.

"FUCK!" protested Meghan as she unlocked her door, dot had gotten all up into her metaphors.

"And good evening to you too. My day was fine, yours?" Lucas had just poured their glass of wine and turned to get another glass, "I didn't expect you 'til way after midnight."

Meghan threw her bag onto the couch and practically ran the three steps of their studio to the kitchen and into Lucas' arms. "Whoa now," was all they could get out before Meghan closed their lips with hers. Lucas knew when they were beat, set the bottle and glass down and pulled Meghan into a deep and backbreaking hug and kiss.

But Meghan didn't release, she drove harder into Lucas' embrace. Finally, they both needed oxygen. Lucas was clearly ready for more, while Meghan grabbed their poured wine glass and drained half of it in one swallow. "Hey now, scolded Lucas, "That's a fine…" they scanned the bottle, "undated… red blend-ish?"

Meghan emptied the glass, "You got this treat a lady right thingy, down." Lucas locked eyes as they refilled the glass, "are we giving Lady and the Tramp all night, or should we drink like adults?" Meghan grabbed the filled glass and turned for the couch, kicking off her heels on the way, "You do you."

Lucas shook their head and refilled the other glass, "So… will words fuck this up?"

Meghan curled up the couch and sipped, she kicked her bag onto the floor making room for Lucas, spilling out her notes. Lucas put their hand to their eyes like blinders, comically pretending not to see the now dishelved pile of her work to date, "It's all about consent."

Meghan sipped again, then jumped up for her notes and returned back onto the couch in one swell foop. Lucas sat. They clinked glasses, each waiting for the other to speak. Meghan reached out and brushed Lucas's bang back across the side fade to behind their ear. Her fingers lingered teasingly on the tip of their ear, they shuddered, eyes closed, then as Meghan caressed down to their lobe, she sighed, “I swear that woman has officially broken over my last line of defense.”

The spell broken, Lucas sighed, and sat up, just a tad salty at having to share this moment with a stranger, they sipped, “So much for professional objectivity.” Meghan opened her notes and turned to Lucas with a raised eyebrow. Lucas shrugged, then nodded, and whispered with surrender, “Consent.” Meghan winked and read aloud, “It wasn’t dot’s carelessness that had brought her down, it was her choice. She had, as she had said, been eating around the middle until she could get to the creamy center. But when she found the center was too much for one woman to ever eat, she knew it was time to switch gears.”

Lucas sipped, expecting more. When none came, they saw Meghan smiling in anticipation. Lucas sipped again, replaying Meghan’s words, hoping for a clue. “Um… is it… milky center?” Meghan shook her head.

“No. It’s hope. This isn’t the end of the line. She’s not done. dot would have never been caught, so whatever she’s still got on her to-do list is going…”

“Never? Countered Lucas, “She would’ve eventually… I mean, you said she admitted it herself, she was going to kill every one of those fuckers… they’re churning out haters like Wonderbread down there, but it’s impossible for one person to stop their fucking machine.”

“She knows something we don’t.”

“Yeah, like how many more she killed, she hasn’t told them

about."

"She's a genius."

"She's a psychopath."

"She's *our* psychopath."

Lucas had finally trundled off to bed after Meghan used their own drool to slick down their ever-cray eyebrows, waking them. They frowned as they stood like a prizefighter who'd been face down on the mat a half breath before… but hey, Meghan smiled to herself, at least their brows were on point. Lucas had staggered forward, kissed her sloppily on the forehead, and teetered off. A bottle of wine will do that to the best of them.

Meghan continued typing. For the first time, her article was to be a feature. With photos. She already had enough material in the week she'd spent with dot for an entire book and they hadn't even gotten to any real details that weren't already known. dot had been quite candid about any question Meghan asked. That was the problem. Meghan had honed her interview skills on the political beat before she was assigned to dot, and she was used to having to pivot on her pivots like a lockpick finessing the tumblers to get to the truth she was seeking. With dot, every question was answered without any subterfuge or nuance, which put Meghan back on her heels every time.

She wasn't used to getting what she asked for.

Ever.

Well, except with Lucas. But they were the exception to every one of Meghan's rules… "Ugh!" The cold coffee was stopped just short of her throat as her entire mouth revolted, shaking her back to the task at hand. She rewound her recording and hit play…

"Were you trying to send a message, dot?"

"No. Meghan. Just like they had no idea I was Transgender until I disclosed it to them, they had no idea it was me until I turned myself in. Since they are incapable of connecting the dots… and don't get me started on the last disaster of Fuckstick Von President and the destruction of our country, messages don't work. Ask Frank Capra, who loved saying "Sam Goldwyn said, If you wanna send a message use Western Union'… that's three references only ten of your readers will get, but… no… I was just eliminating pieces on the chessboard."

"By killing. People are calling you a terrorist."

"Inaccurate."

"How so?"

"A terrorist uses the fear of the possibility of another attack as a tool to coerce or force political or social objectives. I was realistic, I knew their agenda was never going to change no matter what I did. I was executing people."

"Who were state and federal legislators."

"I was whittling down their numbers. They had made it clear

their objective was complete and total erasure of us. They made the decision quite easy."

"It was easy for you?"

"Quite."

Meghan shivered as dot's words transcribed onto her screen. She took out her earbuds and rubbed her eyes. She could remember the crime scenes she had observed. The Nebraska Speaker of the House had just rammed a combined abortion bill and anti-trans "package" in what opponents referred to as a Frankenstein bill, but Nebraskans knew ironically as a Christmas tree bill, through their senate, after a nearly successful total filibuster by one democrat. State Senator Machaela Cavanaugh had stopped the state's debate for over three weeks until she finally agreed to end her stasis of business if the senate agreed to take up only one bill that would discriminate against trans people. (Sacrifices had to be made?) Sen. Cavanaugh has a trans son, so which bill she felt would be acceptable damage became a moot point in the end when both the entire package was co-joined with the anti-abortion bill.

But there was the Speaker. Propped up in his own bed, on the third floor of their Lincoln home, rigor mortis locked hands around a copy of the legislation rolled into a perfect tube which had been rammed down his throat. His eyes were still wide in horror as he lost the ability to stop the penetration, he had, the coroner had surmised, died from choking on his own bile.

It was the Speaker's wife who had found him. The next day. She had been away for the week at a retreat for Republican Nebraskan women. She has been concerned when she didn't get her nightly "goodnight kiss" over the phone, every night for a week. But she just figured "When the cat's away, mice will play," and had no idea how pictures of her husband's last moments got to the internet, despite the FBI's photo embargo. She never knew they were there until after the coroner had taken her husband away.

This was the hardest thing for Meghan to square as she approached her assignment. She just couldn't bring herself to believe the voice and eye she spoke to every day for the last week could be capable of the crimes accused. The Speaker had been over six feet tall, his death a brutally slow wrestling match of sheer strength to which he had finally buckled. Could dot, a woman whom experts were estimating was 60 years old, be that strong?

Meghan had to admit, she had no idea what dot looked like. Even dot's mugshot was no help. State & federal protocols had been ignored or blatantly disregarded, either because the original taker hadn't cared enough to scrutinize their own work, or nobody believed a fair trial was necessary or needed.

Which was as dot has said it would be. We were at war. And in war, humans make other humans inhumane with inhumanity.

The Speaker of the House had been Meghan's first, but it hadn't been dot's.

There were the Las Perlas bouncers in Los Angeles and the

couple who had started the fracas in 2019. Four Latina Trans women were taunted and screamed at in this downtown restaurant bar by a very drunk cisgender couple. When the Latinas responded in kind, the bouncers assaulted the Latinas, putting them in chokeholds and throwing them onto the sidewalk at the club. The club owners never disciplined the bouncers, never apologized for their conduct, and instead, doubled down on the oft-used trope of "men in dresses" assaulting their patrons.

So dot did. Las Perlas burned to the ground one night and while firefighters tamped down the flames they found the owners and the bouncers trapped in the basement bound by chokeholds made of each others' arms. They had their arms tied around each other's with steel cable, but they had all died of smoke inhalation… slowly.

But it was the couple, found in their Mar Vista home that was gruesome. The idyllic calm of this slightly upscale suburban tract was shattered by sirens one Saturday in the wee hours, five years to the day from the original Las Perlas incident. The couple, Doug and Nancy Martin crawled to meet the ambulances with each's severed tongues (cut from each's mouth) sewn to the other's hands. They couldn't even scream. The video of their crawl and the heroic fight to save them by the first responders went viral before they expired, each hemorrhaging the last of their life force onto their manicured lawn. This was the first time anyone had seen the sheet of paper with the three dots connected by a line. But it wasn't recognized as anything of meaning until…

Meghan's cult noticed a partially charred scrap in a photograph of the Las Perla's fire evidence sometime around the investigation of the fifth murder.

"Oh, Yes…" typed Meghan, "There were three more, that we know of, depending on who's counting." Meghan maintained each crime *scene* counted as one, but her editor, Jan Dubrovnik, and Felicia Williams, the writer for the Advocate counted each life lost. But that meant dot's body count (or at least the charges facing her) were up to 47, which always felt like a kick to Meghan's stomach, so she tried to think of it as crime scenes, which only brought it down to 39.

There had been the Governor of Florida, who, having just entered the Presidential race hadn't really gotten his security detail and the Secret Service to play well enough together yet when dot had struck. He was lying in a coma, with no real chance of either a miracle or waking up, which seemed fair enough to dot, "He can't enact his hate agenda when he's unconscious, I'll take the W."

Of course, Meghan knew her own take on things was going to differ from most of the men covering the story, who, as both the FBI & Interpol had all decided when dot had surrendered, had to be part of an army, or hit squad because there was no way one woman, could ever have done this alone.

Of course, right on cue, the white wing (as the conservative "right" wing had come to be known) started speculating that "another radical transgender" serial killer was on the loose. And for once they were actually right. Even a broken clock is right twice a day.

John Thune from the Times gave the most backhanded of compliments when he wrote, "If the rumors are true, which this reporter doubts highly, then the suspect would be like most transgender people had to be in today's world. A classic overachiever."

As a trans woman herself, this was the part that stuck in Meghan's craw the most. And now dot had brazenly confirmed it. This. This was where dot had crossed the line. A trans woman would never have done anything like this, she had argued, when the rumor first started floating around (as they always do without a shred of evidence, despite the shared violence against the Transgender community by the victims).

But when it proved true, it shattered Meghan's worldview.

But not enough to jump off the beat. "If it was one of our own, I have to be the writer." She declared to Jan. And this time Jan agreed.

Meghan stood and stretched. She always had a huge problem with this debate. When do the marginalized get to go back to just being human? Denzel Washington had famously mused he couldn't wait to be able to play the villain, so he could stop having to represent. But Meghan wasn't sure the Trans community was there yet or would ever be.

Maybe instead of listing dot's victims within her article, which would take precious pages to repeat information aggregated by almost every other newsite already, it could be a timeline, sidebar column or a who's who of the hateful, vicious people who had declared, in dot's terms, open war on the trans community and who had been made to pay with their lives. There were soft targets as dot called them; politicians and washed-up rockstars clinging to relevance on the back of innocent people, like the racist bar owner selling 49 cent beers (which was already trolling the Queer community reminding them of the number of victims who had died in the Pulse Nightclub Tragedy) because "he forgot how much fun it was to Poke the Woke." His bar was burned to the ground, and his body was discovered nailed to the bar with full bottles of Bud Light used as nails to pin his arms and legs.

No. Meghan couldn't unsee what she had seen, but she would not martyrize any of them. She would tell Jan that she would only reference the victims when it was relevant to a point she or dot would be making. Some of dot's comments would require context and after all, people want to know what they don't already know, which was…

How.

How, in the fuck…

How in the fucking hell, did one woman do all of this?

How in the fucking hell, one woman did all of this.

Meghan rubbed her eyes and stared at her screen. It had taken four attempts to type that sentence… yes exhausted, but not by her schedule. She sat back and stared at her article. It had consumed all of her like all her work usually does, but this was something…

… something… some… thing…

Like a scab being ripped off and for the slightest of moments you are fascinated by the pink raw flesh before it is flooded by seeping blood, Meghan saw it: the *thing* that had been under the anxiety, fear and malaise she had to claw and fight her way over every waking moment… the backbeat to her nightmares, the throbbing bass line of the outrage that was a mere hairsbreadth from each breath she doled out like a miser to get her through her daily life was this:

The same people, the very same people who flew the American Flag like it was theirs alone, (substituting it for the confederate flag,)…

The very same people who actually believed it was their "God given right" to decide she and her rainbow siblings were less than human, and either actively remove or standing idly by as, the most basic human rights were stripped from her community…

The same people, these very same people who had inflicted actual death and damage to other fellow citizens under the guise of "traditions and beliefs deeply rooted" in "our" American society…

yes, these… same people…

… are the very same people who gave aid & comfort to actual traitors & insurrectionists who tried and failed to stage a coup, to overthrow our fucking government.

The very fucking same people who use the Constitution as shield for every single one of their crimes was the same people who smashed the windows, literally shat on the Speaker of the House's desk, and murdered three, injured many more, and even lost one of their own in the terror attack,

These motherfucking, same people who tried and failed to destroy the sacred Constitution (with ALL of it's flaws) altogether, then…

Have the unmitigated gall to continue to try to use it…

… and are even now trying to whitewash the whole affair – no she would not use words which supported the erasure of their culpability – the *insurrection* from collective memory, the same way they are trying to erase her entire community.

And…

And…

AND…

… it was fucking *working*.

Yes… the tiny shard of glass, the shrapnel imbedded in her mind… the collateral damage the entire country was pretending (and not very well) was something we could eventually heal from, *if we just moved on from it.*

Forgive and forget. “Let bygones be bygones,” “just drop it,” and other things only the guilty and the weak say when ensnared by conscience’s tentacles…

2

“

it’s usually only a handful of men who get to decide to go fuck with someone, war chooses you.

”

Foggy.

Her head and the sky and everything. Meghan had had to be woken up twice. She had used her keyboard for a pillow again, the word “tentacles” was the last coherent word typed followed by the gibberish that her cheek and possibly nose, maybe forehead had attempted to contribute.

Lucas had poured coffee into her as she stood under the spray of water, then had cruelly switched the temperature to the arctic sea setting (which only barely did the trick) and lovingly even drove her to the EL, stuffing the warm roll with vegan butter and another coffee into her backpack as she ascended the steps.

"Hey," they said, turning her into their arms, "If you need me to pick you up at the Pen tonight, I can cancel the dinner."

Meghan's face confirmed what Lucas had already known – she had completely forgotten about their monthly dinner with friends. Lucas kissed her and searched her eyes like a trauma doctor looking for dilation. "Is there even food out there?" Meghan patted her backpack with a smile, "thanks to my guardian angel."

"I'm serious. Just ring me around five and I'll head out. I can work out of the car until you're done." Meghan kissed Lucas and nodded. The eastbound EL thundered into the station, they both clocked it and nodded – the westbound was only seconds away. They hurried in opposite directions.

Safely on the train, Meghan pulled out the coffee and chanced a sip – it was always a risk on the ancient rumbler but it made drinking coffee an adventure.

Yes, she was foggy. But the third dose of caffeine was starting to win this battle. She felt ready to confront her work from the night before. She opened her laptop and reread "the shard," as she decided to label the source of the mental wound which had revealed itself last night, but the blood already scabbed over and she realized her article was not the place for it. She shook her head, this was the exact thing she had railed against, the decision everyone was making daily, to compartmentalize the atrocity of actual treason being committed by even elected leaders to another time when it would be more convenient for some or swept under the rug altogether by others.

Fuck. Meghan hissed aloud. She hated being like everyone else. She placed her cursor at the last paragraphs she had typed last night, highlighting them, but it took almost another 10 stops on the El before she was able to delete them.

She shook it off and got back to work, what remained as the new last paragraphs was…

… a murder she had witnessed firsthand and even at the time felt different from all the others of which she had only seen the forensic photos. It seemed a break in a pattern, a slip? dot's discipline was impeccable, but this looked… in retrospect… sloppy? Or improvised? Rushed, or rather urgent, maybe?

The FBI would take point on this one and stalled in adding to dot's tally until only recently. But Meghan knew it was dot's from the instant she'd heard it across the police scanner, even though it seemed too obvious, too on-the-nose even for dot. The victim was Pastor Daniel Roberts, an Ohio minister with a small but viral congregation.

He had been on the frontlines of the CoVID fights, flaunting the lockdowns openly, despite three super spreader events in the early days before the vaccine had stopped the killing – 29 people died and countless others were infected as congregants had spread out to at least four states. The Minster had lost his wife in the denial and half of his congregation before it was done. But that hadn't stopped the hate.

Maybe in a quest to get back to relevancy, he started with the anti-trans sermons, misquoting bible verses, calling on "Good Christians" to rid the country of "this blight of mental illness." And the town had delivered a trans teen named Kel McMullins, to their cause, kidnapping him from school one day to prove conversion therapy could work. Three days of deprivation, "prayer" and other unspeakable acts of their conversion therapy ended…

… with Kel taking his 15-year-old life.

When Pastor Dan was found two weeks after being reported missing the day of Kel's funeral, it seemed in a whole other league than dot's work. Meghan had thought long and hard about her description before she typed, "It was unique in its brutality, pointing to a more personal motive than the somewhat more pun-ish, and let's face it, theatrical tableaus previously attributed to, and now claimed by dot…"

But Meghan struggled to write what she had seen. She had arrived on the scene before the police. The scanner was coming in handy, this time the incident was local, in her own backyard, relatively, which proved to be a double-edged sword.

Like the Las Perlas couple, tortured death was the point, timed to be kept alive long enough for someone, possibly a camera, to watch them die. Pastor Dan had been found near a barn in

Illinois, three states away from his Ohio home. A bible, soaked in fuel had been used as an igniter, hellfire flames had seared the book to his chest over his heart consuming the facial skin instantly, before also consuming the rest of the body's skin, effectively skinning the Pastor alive. With his tortured flesh gone, nerves exposed, life and blood seeping out in a slow but steady trickle, he managed to crawl on a gravel path in a last gasp for help.

Meghan had seen the corpse-like form trying to crawl as she jumped from her rented car but was quickly frozen by horrified disbelief, her mind just would not let her understand what she was seeing. It, the corpse tried to speak to her, and she was almost through working up the courage to walk forward and at least acknowledge this creature as human when sirens and chaos exploded behind her. Whoever had called this one in had made it known the cavalry had better show up.

Instantly a storm of earnestness and activity swept past her and circled the creature. Firefighters had smelled the fuel and the accelerant, "PENTRITE!" and immediately cordoned off the area. The creature groaned in pain and confusion. The TV cameras had picked it up before anyone who understood what was happening. Once the safety of the first responders had been set, they turned once again to the still alive, still writhing in unspeakable pain pile of Pastor, and rolled him over. His eyes no longer had muscles or skin to hold them so they rolled out of their sockets and stretched to the ground even as the face was pointed at the sky. Meghan still remembered even in his last moments he wasn't even able to appeal to heaven.

A quick-thinking cop had stepped up with his iPhone to look at the smoldering rectangle in the center of the chest, "It's a goddamned bible." He snapped a pic and bend closer to look… we got any bible toters, what's… Matthew 5:22?"

As others had fumbled around for a bible, the cop took more pictures. Meghan had been the only one to notice the body had stopped quivering and had gone still. One of the ambulance drivers stepped up with his pocket bible and started reading to the cop who turned his iPhone on him and recorded it, "But I say to you, everyone who is angry with his brother shall be guilty before the court; and whoever says to his brother, 'You good-for-nothing,' shall be guilty before the supreme court; and whoever says, 'You fool,' shall be guilty enough to go into the fiery hell."

Meghan can still hear how his words, quaking in the late afternoon stillness, amid the smell of chemicals and burned flesh blending with the columbines and alfalfa, *felt* like when he stopped reading. In the eerie calm, everyone seemed to finally notice...

... the Pastor had expired.

Found *guilty enough* before a crowd of his peers, for the fate that had been rendered. Meghan had sobbed openly. Others couldn't help but join in. She couldn't even remember getting home.

"And… is there a question in there?"

Meghan raised her head, she had been staring at her shoes… as the cold and dank of dot's anti-cell wrapped its tentacles around her skin, she came back fully into her own awareness. dot's eye stared unblinking from the dingy window of the cell door, waiting… for an answer.

Meghan stammered… cleared her throat… she stopped. She stared at dot's eye. She held the stare. She tried to unclench her grasp on her disorientation, she was here, so her morning's commute was successful, her purpose for being here… that was the cloudy part… the stench of the Pastor's last moments clung to her awareness like a bad hangover… and yet…

"People will need to know how."

"And yet your heart needs to know why?"

Neither had blinked in this new eternity. Meghan's weakness had given her resolve. But dot was as fascinated as she was compassionate. Her stare softened, but it remained steady, a reassuring, gentle calm, "Meghan, do you wish to sit?"

Meghan continued to stare, "I feel like you are evading my question… which is a first for our conversations."

"You have finally asked a question worth answering, but it's not a simple one. You will grow wearier than you already are."

"I… thank you… for your concern, but I am fine."

"The how is always different. Are you asking about the Pastor's murder alone?"

"Let's start there. I was present… I saw his death… so I know what you…"

"Good as any. What would you like to know?"

"It… felt rushed… improvised almost… you seemed…"

"Oh God no. It did need to happen in a timely manner, there was no way I was going to let the fucker say anything at or around that dear boy's funeral. I would not have him pulling focus from the boy and his family's life. None of these were rushed. They take weeks to study and plan, I'm not a natural-born killer. And the goal… well, If I'm caught, how can I complete the mission?"

"Which is?"

"Another excellent question…

I suppose that's why I'm here, I'm reevaluating the mission. But, we digress… you asked me how. The Pastor like most men is so arrogant he makes many mistakes. He truly orders his life as if it is never under threat, unlike us who have grown-up looking over our shoulders, dancing between raindrops, trying desperately, despite how evolved we are, to not get clocked, no, these are the easiest ones but they're also low-hanging fruit, low-value targets, they think they own the world. So, after mapping out his schedule and movements, I learned the Pastor likes a glass of brandy before bed. I used a slow-acting sedative, which kept him asleep in the morning long after his wife got up for her day, and she, the ever dutiful wife thought he 'needed his sleep'. "

"You're right, I will need that chair." Meghan slumped onto the metal chair and took out her notebook, "How did you know his wife wouldn't notice anything in the morning?"

"She's pretty confident that 'the Lord protects,' so she goes about her day obliv to any but the most obvious things in her world. And I just needed it to be a seamless extraction to give me the most time to accomplish his end. I ran the shower so she would hear things in the expected order and the sound gave me a little more cover to remove him from the house. Unlike the Speaker, the point was to remove the walls of safety of the castle they thought was impenetrable."

"But how'd you get in, in the first place?"

"I was in before they came home from church."

"Church? But… I thought… wait, church the day before?"

"Of course. It's the best time. The Pastor's house was empty every Sunday from 7:00 am to afternoon at the very least."

"So, you were in the house the entire day and night?"

"Yes, but this is not the most interesting detail is it?"

"Interesting? You sound like you enjoy this."

"Enjoy taking a life? Murdering someone. No. That's what makes us different. There's no joy in killing these people who relish eliminating us from society. Just like them, we are born every minute, and we are trying to do everything we can so our children can enjoy life. Free from fear. Free from hatred."

"You said we. I thought you were working alone?"

"I am. It's really the only way. When there's others involved, you have to care for them too. And that's where discipline wobbles."

"So, then who is we?"

"You, me, our community, everyone under the ever-growing and expanded wing of T."

Meghan considered protesting. She wasn't signing on to murder on behalf of anyone, but instead, heard her mouth say, "But you took the Pastor across three states, which was weird because that takes a lot of logistics; you have to have had a team supporting you."

"It'd be nice, but, again, everyone has their own life. I can't ask anyone to have the same level of commitment as me. It's my idea, and I'm the only one who I can reasonably ask and expect to commit body & soul to it."

Meghan realized she hadn't been recording, "Fuck." She started digging in her backpack for her recorder, when she succeeded in finding and extracting it she turned it on and noticed dot was no longer staring out her cell, "Um… sorry. I'm ready again."

From the back of the cell, dot replied, "Which answer do you need repeating?" Meghan stared out the dirty sliver of a window into the gray skies, "Everyone eventually understood the bible stuff but why Illinois? What was the significance of the barn?"

"Honestly, it was convenience. I had gotten that barn for a

decent price and had been thinking about a farm-to-table kinda restaurant thingy, but I just hadn't gotten around to it."

Meghan shook her head, "A… thingy?"

"Yes, you know, a destination restaurant, more of an experience, closer to the earth, locavore vibe. But most of my bigger plans have all been backburnered since the war ramped up."

"War? You think you're at war with…"

"Oddly, We, as Americans have this weird entitled thing with war, we believe we get to choose when and if we're at war. Most of humankind doesn't ever get a say if they want to be at war. It's usually only a handful of men who get to decide to go fuck with someone. War chooses you."

Meghan scribbled in her notebook. dot continued, "In the trans community, there's some, I call them virtues, makes us different from cis folx, one of them is we don't push when we ask anything of someone. It's not an always thing but, you never know where someone is in their transition, you can't know what they've already had to overcome to get where they are, and if they're even ready for more or anything else. You can ask but you have to be able to hear their no."

Meghan's eyebrows furrowed. "So, Meghan are you in our war?"

Meghan shivered, "Will it change what we're doing here?"

"Do you really think I would've agreed to this with a cis

reporter?"

"I don't remember telling anyone I was Trans."

"Girl."

Meghan bristled.

"Are your feathers up because you feel you've been outed, in which case… Girl. Or are your feathers up because a white woman appropriated the term Girl… in which case… *girl*?"

Meghan chewed on the inside of her cheek, smiling slightly as she weighed clapping back against how much more she needed to write the feature, "Girl. I don't feel outed, but I do… want to maybe know how they described me to you. And yes, it felt… very *white lady* of you to hear you bust out, *girl*."

"Noted. I apologize. It was their idea to have me interviewed. And I saw only a pool of approved potential news *websites* from which to choose. I told them I would only talk to you. And you alone. So…"

"So…what… you wouldn't be this… talkative if I had been a cis person?"

"Meghan, dear. It's about trust. You may not write a flattering piece on me, but at least I can trust you'll understand what I'm saying."

Meghan stood to stretch her legs and shake off the adrenaline, "You can trust I'll be fair."

"Another trans overachiever."

"Is there any other way?"

"Not for us."

"So…"

"So… I guess you'll have to reckon with why you were the chosen."

Meghan tried to ignore the cold shiver that ripped through her body. The muscle memory of being outed in the days before her coming out. The icy-hot feeling of being stripped naked in public, alone, and vulnerable. She was out, everywhere. Now, loved and accepted, respected, even. She hadn't had to deal with the hatred and discrimination that surrounded seventy percent of her community affected her daily *personal* life – it had all been a war she had been able to keep at a privileged distance with her career, and progressive life. She could abstract it, compartmentalize it, keep it at bay, while believing she was "fighting the good fight."

She stared at her notes. An insignificant pool noodle in the tsunami sweeping her very far from shore.

"So… you… snuck… the Pastor out of his house and drove him three states away to a farm you owned. Were you concerned the farm might get traced back to you?"

"The farm isn't listed to me on the title, so there was less on the ol' to-do' list than a standard operation. This one was more about timing plus I had to keep the ol' Pastor occupied for almost two weeks…"

"Because? Why did you wait two weeks?"

"Because I needed at least that much time for Kel's parents to grieve before the focus would shift to the Pastor, he would be considered a victim and his death would eclipse Kel's and his parents didn't deserve that."

"Is this regret coming from dot?"

"Is this sarcasm coming from Meghan?"

"I'm sorry… I apologize. It caught me off guard."

"All of these factors had to go into every strike. We are all, Trans & cis, one human family. None of us is expendable. I'm just trying to stop them from killing us. And I think that's another thing where we're different. I know and acknowledge my actions are going to end in someone's death, I am upfront about that. Also, I know who's going to die. I am not a coward, I look every one of them in the eye and tell them in no uncertain terms why they are dying. Their actions have brought them these consequences. It's not some grandiose cosmic karmic thing. It's simple cause and effect."

"Does it make you feel powerful?"

"Powerful? No, my actions have chained me to these consequences too. Once war comes to you there are only two choices from then on. Surrender or victory. And surrender rarely goes well."

"But it sounds like you aren't taking responsibility for entering the war. That was a choice, was it not?"

"I suppose I could've pretended the war would go away. But that would be incredibly naive. I am white and as cliche'd as it is, I am middle-aged, so I am now also invisible, and we can talk about that when you get more age under that belt of yours, but honey, the Anti-trans hate /war machine is a real thing, and I can't ignore it, can YOU??? And yes, hearing my own words echo off the cell walls, I do sound like I'm playing a victim card in a game of responsibility. But, after I turned 60…"

Meghan scribbled in her notebook.

"Let me know when you're done."

Meghan raised her eyes slowly, "You wanted that noted, that wasn't a slip of the tongue. Are you proud of your age?"

"Should I be?"

"Well, I think people thought you had to be a lot younger."

"A sixty-year-old woman wasn't capable of all of this. Yup. Another place where we're different from our cis-sters. We have a more optimistic view of what humans are capable of. Maybe it comes from second puberty. But anyway, once I turned 60, I did start to realize it would never stop of its own accord, this war on us. After that spring when it seemed the only thing they knew how to do was hate -- hate us through legislature, which inspired hate through real intimidation and violence, I couldn't sit on the sidelines, anymore. War came to my heart."

"You're not being metaphorical. You really believe this."

"That's not a question, Meghan."

"Yes, our lives can suck and it weighs on me every day, but it's not my whole life."

"Well, you have that privilege and that's great. It's what we're fighting for. But our babies haven't been trained to live and thrive despite the hate. They're having to figure it out while they're dodging bullets"

"Just like we did."

"It wasn't like this. The enemy's toxic beliefs have torched the atmosphere, creating a cloud over us all. Saying the quiet part out loud is now a feature, not a bug and it is affecting our babies. They grow up with people actually *trained* to hate us, people who don't even question the logic of their parents."

dot put both her eyes to the glass and locked them with Meghan. She continued.

"I used to believe love would conquer all, and the dirty little secret is they always believed that too, so their plan is to destroy love before it can even have a chance. They take away any love or connection be it through our teachers, our doctors or our communities… clever, huh?"

“Oof. That’s incredibly pessimistic.”

“Call me Pollyanna. But seriously girl, you can see what they’re trying to achieve.”

“And did you tell this to the Pastor?”

“No. He wasn’t worth the breath. I kept him in a coma until his day came.”

“Which was…?

“When Kel’s parents went on vacation. That was the only real significance of the day. I wanted them as far away from the fracas as possible. They were in the air when the Pastor’s last moments went viral, and I had hoped the FBI would scrub it as soon as they discovered the yahoo who had broken the embargo. It worked. And enough people saw it to make it effective, sorry, I know you like using meaningful, but I wanted to make sure it happened while Kel’s parents were too busy healing in a Buddhist temple in Angor Wat to open their phones. It was the best I could’ve hoped for.”

“Why was it important to be effective?”

“None of these assholes ever worked alone. In Kel’s case, there were three motherfuckers who helped with the torture. That boy was kid-fucking-napped. He was tortured and harassed for three days, they actually tried to waterboard him! A fucking teenager saw how to do it on YouTube and thought it might work to get Kel to renounce WHO HE FUCKING WAS! The poor child. Kel was destroyed the moment he understood that *this was how much he was hated.*

He was broken then and there.

That's what's breaking our babies, and who could blame them? It's not the what or even the how, it's the why. We all have asked ourselves why. Why would we want to share this earth with someone as hideous, as inhuman as them? Why would anyone want for even a second to pretend these cruel, cis cretins have any right to coexist with us?"

"Are you calling for their extermination, Ms. Hitler?

"Calling for it? They had already declared it. So… I had to start the process."

"But we were talking about being effective."

"Yes. It was going to take a fuck all amount of time to get everyone with Kel's blood on their hands, once the police got activated by the Pastor's death. It was too risky to try something with everyone's guard up, so I would have to rely on the toxins released in their bodies by their fear of their own chickens coming home to roost to erode them from inside out.

"I thought sending messages didn't work?"

"Oh, I'm not sending a message. I'm letting them marinate in their own fear."

"You sound more like a serial killer every day."

"Just saying the quiet part out loud."

"Whatever you have to tell yourself. Which brings up a another point…"

"You're okay with these tangents? 'Cuz it is getting late for you and you haven't asked me what has been eating you all this time. You don't want to have another night like you had last night."

Meghan checked her watch. dot was right. "How do you know what my night was like last night?"

"Meghan."

"Fine. Yes. It sounds like this one really affected you. Did you know Kel? Or the Pastor? Is that why it was so… fucked up? So… horrifying?"

dot's eye appeared at the window, "They all affect me like that. There is a real sense that what I'm doing is completely senseless, it will never bring our children back. And I feel their loss in the pit of my heart. It shreds me from the inside out. All of my rationales; that it will make it better for the future, that it might save one child, are endlessly empty reasons. All I can do with this anguish is hope that I balance the scales a bit, but even that is bullshit.

I don't believe that karma will even this out, but I do believe in karma and my own hand in mine. And I know that if I let their actions go without answer I myself would disappear into my own sense of senselessness. So, I'm settling for the reduction of the enemy one soldier at a time. The Pastor needed to know that he would not be going to the heaven he prayed to, in the name of his God. His people needed to have their doubt cleave them from the faith they used as a shield from their own actions. And I needed them to know that now, so that they didn't harm anyone, least of all, our siblings, ever again."

"But, won't they just retaliate? What's stopping them from succumbing to their fear like they always do, exploding from their rage like you did? What if this sets off yet another endless fucking cycle of violence? It will be because of you.

"Fair point. But, I don't think this will go that way. I can almost guarantee it…"

"Guarantee? That's arrogant. Not like you. How do you guarantee it?"

"That wasn't the end of that mission."

"What does that mean?"

"When will your story be posted?"

"Why, are you afraid my article will tip them off to…"

dot's eye receded into the gloom.

Meghan stopped the recorder.

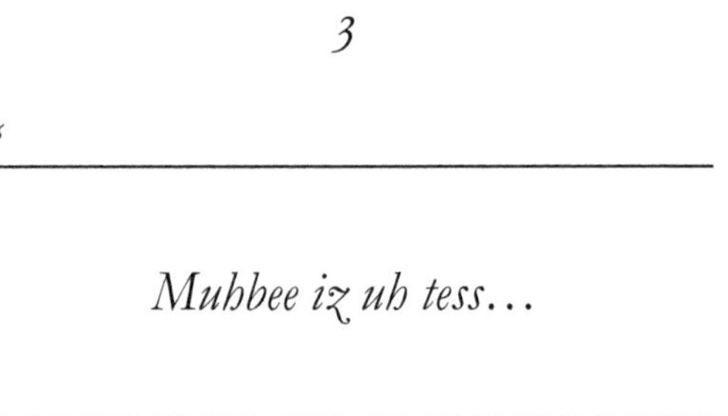

Meghan stepped into the misty night. She was in a new fog. One created by the dark and sticky dreck that had flooded her system mere moments before. There hadn’t even been a goodnight. Just silence for several seconds that was finally shattered by the opening of the steel door. Meghan had scooped up her belongings and hadn’t even put on her coat or stashed her notebook and recorder in her backpack until she stood before the desk clerk who returned her iPhone and keys, then nodded to the guard at the door who buzzed her out.

Meghan read her phone as Lucas ran up to her from the parking lot, “I thought something must be wrong, so I came.”

Meghan jumped into their arms and started shaking. Lucas squeezed her tight, “Are you crying?” Meghan pulled away from Lucas to show her face and shuddered from toe to head like a rope that had been cracked at one end, “No. Just… cold. Very cold.”

Lucas led her to their vintage pick-up truck. Its candy-apple red paint job appeared a murky purplish brown under the lone sodium vapor light hanging on for dear life on the rusty pole. Meghan took her place on the bench seat next to Lucas as they started the car, cranked the heater, and headed onto the highway.

They had driven several miles on the country highway before Lucas thought it was safe to ask her how she was doing. She had clung to them for the entire trip and she had only just now stopped shivering. “You okay?”

She snuggled deeper into their shoulder and squeezed them reassuringly. Lucas glanced into the rearview mirror at Meghan, Take all the time you need, Babe. But… I am a little hungry, though. You cool if we stop at Felipe’s?”

Meghan met their gaze, “Pizza? I could eat a whole pie.” Lucas smiled, their girl was coming back.

They drove in silence until they hit the interstate and headed for Chicago. Meghan kissed Lucas on the cheek and slid across the bench to grab her backpack, she took out her notebook and scribbled a few notes and then slid back across the bench and snuggled up to Lucas, "She was in rare form today. Basically, she's at war on all our behalf."

Lucas let her words sink in. "War… well she's not wrong. How the hell is she going to be able to get a fair trial? To us, she's a folk hero, and to the cis world, she's living proof of every lie they tell their children…" Meghan shuddered again, "And they ain't too far off the mark about that." The windshield was starting to collect the gloomy mist, and Lucas turned on the wipers, "What's her defense?"

Meghan shook her head, "That's the problem, she doesn't have any. She has no remorse, she's very thoughtful, very calculating, measured… she makes sense until you remember she's talking about murder. She doesn't whine like some wannabe terrorist, there's no manifesto or screed. They are killing us, so she is killing them. It's how everyone you've ever known who's actually been to war, talks about it."

Lucas changed lanes, "Sounds like you are starting to respect her?" Meghan turned the heater down, "I'm starting to understand her. She is truly committed to her plan, You know how when you decided to transition and you knew you were going to do some radical things to your body, even though it was scary and involved some radical medical intervention, you hit that point when you stopped even thinking about what if and you thought only of what, when?"

Lucas smiled, "You mean that point when not even what your father thinks or will do when he finds out, is as scary as *not* doing it?" Meghan hugged Lucas, "Yeah. Well, that's how she talks about what she's doing. "

"Yeah, Babe. I have to admit, I have to keep reminding myself she's murdering people. And a lot of Trans Folx are pissed, they say she's making it harder. Scaring cis people is a dangerous play."

Meghan turned to face Lucas, "And what does Lucas say?" Lucas sighed, "I can see their point, but really what's different? Cis people never needed an excuse to fuck with us before, and they're gonna whine and complain if they were hung with a new rope."

"What's that supposed to mean?"

Lucas laughed, "It's something my dad used to say. I think he meant that people gonna complain no matter how good they got it."

Meghan continued to stare at them with folded arms.

Lucas caught on, "And… I say, go dot? I mean I don't like the killing part, but those who died will never fuck with anyone again, so… there's that. You?"

Meghan uncrossed her arms and returned to her snuggle position, "I said all that and more to her today. I don't know what is going to make these assholes stop with the daily onslaught. Between legislating us out of public life and cutting off access to health care it's like they really do think they can erase us from life and then what? We will just stop existing? Our babies are born every minute!!!! We've always been here and we will always be here.

Do they actually think that some social contagion magically turned us all Trans? Made us suddenly appear?"

"We were always here."

"That's right. We. Were. Always. Here. And there are cis folx who hate us, really, really hate us. And it doesn't seem that that's going to change in time to save the next Trans person from violence. But… I mean, I don't think I could kill anyone ever. And I don't wanna live in a world where I'm constantly looking over my shoulder…"

"You mean like now? I don't walk into any room with confidence anymore. You never know who's gonna go all Target Pride collection on my ass. I mean people are thrashing the stores, knocking over everything that's got a rainbow, mannikins the whole thing. And Target's answer is that they are pulling stuff back under the guise of protecting their employees. Megs, they are winning, It's so fucking fucked!"

An hour had flown by without either of them noticing its passing. Lucas pulled into the late-night pizza hang and found it ghostly quiet. "Well, honey it is a school night," reminded Meghan as she got out of the truck, "no lines…"

They entered and the smell of pizza sauce, baked garlic, and oregano practically line danced into their senses, immediately lifting their mood. Lucas sauntered to the counter, and gestured over their shoulder to Meghan, "How 'bout a vegan pie for the Lady and I'll have the carnivore chaos."

The teenager behind the counter snarked, "Performative much?"

Lucas grinned, "For the right price." The teenager bowed with mock surrender, "Coming right up, *Sir.*" Lucas clocked the "Ask me my pronouns" button on the teenager's lapel and nodded, "Maybe they need to print that button upside down so you can read it too."

The teenager spun and snapped the ticket on a line that stretched across the kitchen window, then spun back, "My pronouns are She/They, what are yours?" Lucas nodded, "My pronouns are they/them." The teenager looked Lucas up and down and then to Meghan, who replied "She /Her. And can we still get a couple of beers?" The teenager gestured to the clock behind them on the wall, "Yes, you've still got an hour. What'll it be?"

Lucas raised an eyebrow, "Well the Lady will want a Goose Island, and I'll have…." They studied the row of taps, then answered "I guess a Goose, too."

The teenager nodded and gestured to the dining area, "Have a seat."

Meghan had already ducked into the booth and was scribbling in her notebook. Lucas slid in beside her, "Have you warmed up enough to talk about it?" Meghan finished her note, and kissed them on the cheek, "You are just the absolute best." She kissed them on the lips and pressed against their whole face as if drawing strength from them. Lucas pulled her in closer, wrapping their arms around her and engulfing her. From deep within their arms, Meghan cooed, "Mmm, okay, I take it all back, you don't spend too much time in the gym." Lucas smiled under her smooch.

They felt the teenager before they saw them, standing with a tray a respectful distance away, waiting. Lucas unwrapped their arms from Meghan and she straightened her hair, "Sorry, it's been… a day." The teenager set the tray down and placed a pitcher between them and two glasses, "It's on the house. Thanks for keeping me 100." Lucas poured for them both, "Oh, that's cool, we get it. No worries. But we can pay for it, seriously you don't need to do that."

Meghan grabbed her beer and held it up to toast the teenager, "Yeah, I'd imagine that would be coming out of your paycheck. Seriously, you don't need to do that."

The teenager grabbed the tray, "Thanks but I own the place, and we have high standards here and when we fuck up, we learn and make ourselves even better. So, enjoy."

Lucas shrugged and raised their glass. Meghan answered, and they lifted them high to the teenager and sipped. The beer filled Meghan with a warmth that worked immediately. Lucas took another swallow and set down their beer, "So you were saying?"

Meghan sipped again, "It's a professional dilemma, what if you knew someone was going to hurt someone else and you didn't stop it?" Lucas nodded to the teenager, "Well actually I was talking about working out, but…"

Meghan followed Lucas' gaze, "No you clown, you asked me if I was ready to talk." Lucas almost spit his beer, "Yeah, yes I did. What made you so cold? That was, I'm not gonna lie, fucking scary. You were chilled like, haunted house chilled."

"dot's going to strike again, and I know who."

Lucas drained his beer and poured another, "Isn't there something like reporter client confidentiality?"

Meghan, "Yes and no. But… that doesn't make it right. I think she was telling me that something has been set in motion already, it will happen even though she's locked away in a prison."

The teen returned with the pizzas and plates and utensils. Lucas examined the bamboo fork, "We've been coming here for years and we never knew you owned the place." The teen handed them shakers of parmesan, another one labeled VEGAN and another with dried red pepper, "I get that all the time, my parents wanted me to learn the value of money, so the family pooled their money together for a loan and here we are. I paid 'em all back so I didn't have to take their 'suggestions' anymore."

Lucas and Meghan snapped their fingers in acknowledgment, Lucas raised their slice as if toasting "Best pie. But who's Felipe?" The teen sighed, "The most clichéd name I could think of, I was going to go with Luigi's but they've got 6 stores before I got it together, so… Felipe's it was. Can I get you anything else?"

With mouths full they both merely shook their heads and the teen left. Meghan looked around, "I… can't believe I had bought into the whole… I didn't even think about who owned this place or… fuck, any of it."

Lucas, mouth still full of pizza said, "We all judge books by their covers. Acknowledge, apologize, and move on." Meghan raised her slice to toast Lucas, "Don't leave me hanging." Lucas rolled their eyes and touched their mangled slice to Meghan's, "Do you want to warn whoever she's going after?"

"Want…?" Well, I feel obligated to protect life. I mean, you say it all the time, if we do it like they do aren't we just as bad?"

Lucas wiped their mouth, "How weird. We would be just as bad. Not better. Not worse. Almost like the same or equal or something."

Meghan grabbed another slice, "Funny. This is serious. The Queer community has only ever been able to achieve any of our gains because we were able to turn hearts and minds because our cause was just. It was undeniable. Bystanders became Allies when they could see that we were actually being oppressed. And cooler heads prevailed. When we applied the WWGD doctrine, we went forward."

Lucas stopped, "WWGD?"

Meghan rolled her eyes, "What Would Ghandi Do."

Lucas swallowed, "You're making that up. Most people can't even spell Ghandi, but I get your point. But don't forget the civil rights movement succeeded with equal parts Dr. Martin Luther King, and Malcolm X."

Meghan stopped, "Get the Latinx Non-Binary person lecturing the Black Trans woman about Martin & Malcolm." Lucas snatched the pizza from her hand, "My trauma can beat your

trauma every day."

"Na'uh,"

"Uh huh"

"Na'uh"

"Uh huh!"

They both laughed and rolled into each other with hands full of pizza. Meghan took a sip of beer, "What I can't figure out is why she's so willing to be so open."

Lucas stared down at their now empty tray, "Hey, there was a full pizza here a second ago! Uh, didn't you say her mission hasn't been completed? There's no way she's going to be able to control the narrative when she's on the stand, she's using you to get it right.

Meghan slid the last two pieces of the vegan pie over to Lucas, "Well, that part's obvious, but why would she tell me that there's going to be something more…?"

Lucas happily scooped up both pieces of pie and slapped them together like a sandwich, "Maybe she slipped up, because of your mad interrogation skills."

Meghan drained her beer. "She doesn't slip."

Lucas took a huge bite, "Muhbee iz uh tesss."

Meghan wiped the sauce from Lucas's chin and waited patiently for them to finish chewing and swallow. They grinned sheepishly, choked it down, then coughed out "Maybe it's a test, she's seeing if she can trust you, or what you'll do?"

Meghan shrugged, it was the best she had as fatigue took the front seat in her brain.

4

"

The fourth is time…

"

Lucas had tucked Meghan in sometime after midnight. She'd have one more day of interviews before she had to turn in her outline to her editor. Last night at Felipe's had been more than her usual dates with Lucas, in that they usually hashed out fixing the world, but something was ringing in her ears that something significant had happened, although she had been too tired to have understood. She resolved to let it settle in her consciousness and continue to mull it later.

As Meghan rattled on the EL out of the city she tried to get a jump on turning in her pages. She never liked working this way, preferring instead to let it all mix together with all her thoughts until she would "vomit it all onto the page" in a two-day torrent, then edit it over the course of a another two days of no sleep, no shower and Lucas pouring coffee and food into her when they could get her to open her mouth.

But that was when she was working on her masters's before she turned professional.

At this point, she was only sure of what she didn't know. But her editor Jan was old school and would be grilling her about the finer points, and only if they were on the page. Meghan had had a rocky start with Jan, trying to shuffle off her outline with generic bullet points, believing that turning in a great article at the last minute would save her. When Jan didn't accept her article because it didn't have what they had agreed to with the outline, Meghan was devastated but knew she had had it coming. She never made that mistake again.

But she still had an outline to write and her 'hunches had to have bunches' of facts to back 'em up, as Jan was fond of saying. And Meghan had none.

She looked over her notes, plotting out her day with dot, and resolved to get something better together for Jan than the lame vagueness that stared back at her from her notepad.

Meghan also resolved to be alert to all of the details swirling around her as she checked in at the Pen. She was still getting used to surrendering her iPhone every day, not that she'd need it and she'd have to admit, less screen time was feeling good. She noticed that the same guard that always stood watch as she dealt with the clerk had stubble, "Must be at the end of his shift, rather than the beginning," She thought.

Growing up Trans had trained Meghan to usually be hyper-observant of people in mundane situations, she imagined that dot was a master at this — a defense mechanism turned skillset. 'Why was she just now seeing all this?' became the predicate of every thought, 'This place has seen better days, why was she just now seeing this?' 'Someone had literally painted on the walls, 'No posting on walls, why was she just now seeing all this?' Meghan was instantly aware of how *unaware* she had been for the last almost 2 weeks.

She tried to let herself off the hook. When she had first walked in here almost two weeks ago, she was overwhelmed, trying desperately to figure out why she had been selected. Yes, it was her secret passion. Yes she had spent the better part of a year chasing this story – BUT nobody but her fellow culties (as they started jokingly referring to themselves) knew-knew.

When Jan explained that the Stateville Warden had personally called for her, Meghan nearly fainted. Jan chalked it up to her steady reputation for thought provoking well-researched sober reporting. All true, but she couldn't bring herself to confess her pre-existing "obsession" with the case.

And still hadn't…

When she had actually walked through the door into the Pen, her survival mode had exploded around her like an airbag in a head-on collision. She pulled herself into the protective shell of her body, not even allowing the light from her eyes to shine out, becoming as invisible as one could be.

She had been here before. Not the Pen, but a place even worse. On her 21st birthday, no less. When the local sheriff had decided that her blood alcohol content, tho' on the border of being illegal, warranted a harrowing 'life-lesson,' which included being thrown into the men's side of the county jail for 9 days; a place the guards lovingly called, 'Gladiator School.'

So yeah, she was, as the kids like to say, triggered.

'Could you blame her?' Meghan asked herself as if third person reference would allow her the benefit of hindsight with its 20/20 promise.

She felt the mild rush that comes with epiphany, the gentle waking up that came with being slightly more comfortable with the mundane choreography of checking in at the Pen, and hoped it would wash the guilt, shame, regret that came with having been sleepwalking in place where she knew only too well, how 'at risk' she had been.

In the time it took to process Meghan's badge, she resolved to nurture her awakened awareness rather than rabbithole into her guilt. She saw how the guard had a few tics that belied a disdain for his job, despite the oppressive air of authority, she had only seen before. He would stare at women, but look away when they caught him staring. He touched his face when he stared at a woman and he never seemed to inhale, only exhaling with an audible grunt.

"I hope you're getting what you need, let me know if that monster gives you any trouble," said the clerk as she slid Meghan's badge under the bulletproof glass. Meghan saw for the first time the wall of video monitors behind her, showing thirty angles of the Pen from the outside, several near the entrance showed a small group of heavily armed protestors waving signs and shouting. Meghan affixed the badge to her peacoat, "What's the protest?"

The clerk glanced over her shoulder, "Been here for the last three days. Some idiot posted that your Girl was here. They don't work here anymore, buh bye."

"Three days?" This waking up shit was even deeper than Meghan thought.

"Yeah, there's only about 20 or thirty of 'em. If you don't come up the main entrance you probably never seen 'em. There's less of them every day."

"Well," Meghan nodded graciously, "Thank you. See you on the other end."

"Not the way these clowns pay overtime." Meghan shrugged and nodded and turned to face the guard. He stuck out his hand for the badge and thrust it under the scanner as if demonstrating how technology was taking his job. He thrust it back to Meghan and stepped aside crisply to allow her to walk through the gate as it rattled down its tracks like an old steam engine in a Western movie.

Meghan was blown away at how she hadn't taken in the Pen

before. But this time was different, she was on a field trip, no longer worried about her own safety, she scrutinized everything, studied everyone, looked everyone in the eye, and categorized them, friend, foe, obstacle, possible ally…

… just as she had trained herself before and during her transition. It was fear-based when she first started it, a way to clock the clockers. Was she safe in this area? Safe in that place? It was exhausting, but it was necessary she believed, and other girls believed it too, and it was something that didn't go away fully until after her bottom surgery. And then it went away completely. Poof! Forty years of fear, confusion, anxiety, pain, and suffering vanished as soon as the anesthesia wore off. And with it, the defense mechanisms she had carefully nurtured since her teens.

Meghan wouldn't even let her awareness break the spell, she'd dig into why this arrow had just returned to her quiver (without the pain) later, but right now it was almost exhilarating, and she decided to let it ride…

dot was housed on the 7th floor of a 7-floor wing of the Pen. Meghan had never looked up from the bottom before. What she saw was a fuck of a high stack of iron bars and concrete walls and floors. Cold, glacier-like inside an iron cage. Cold faces with cold eyes stared at her as she ascended the stairs with a cold guard leading the way.

After seven flights of stairs, she passed an elevator door. It opened when another guard got out, nodded to Scruffy the Guard and kept going in the opposite direction. Meghan studied her guard, their eyes swallowed her question with a blank stare. Meghan smiled to herself, "I get it. They're hazing me. Big surprise there. But she couldn't resist, asking aloud, "How many steps do you need today?"

"Still shy 'bout fifteen hunert."

"You're welcome."

"Than… ks."

The lightning crack and buzz of the solenoid growling in protest interrupted, as the opening of the steel door to the anti-cell of dot's enclosure. Meghan waited for the door to fully open, before turning to bid the guard goodbye and stepped in, "Good afternoon dot."

"Welcome back, Meghan. I trust you wish to get right into it?"

Meghan sat at the bench and methodically pulled her tools from her backpack in keeping with her refreshed attitude of the day; recorder, notebook, pen. She started the recording, uncapped the pen, took a breath, "Yes, but… are you aware that there's been protestors here for the last three days?"

"Oh, yeah. The morning guard thought he was the next best thing. I had reminded them that any sort of shenanigans would trigger an instant change of venue and Chicago wants this one real bad. So the DA made it a condition of surrender, no pictures or news. That guard who posted will never work in this town ever."

“How do you know so much about people?”

“How do you NOT know so much about people?”

“Well…”

“Meghan, honey. The later you transition, the more you *only* have the study of your fellow humans to feel alive. You know this. It’s both a survival skill and balm for the self-inflicted wounds from being in the closet. It’s the study for a someday that you never really believe will come. It’s the person you would’ve been or maybe might be, compared and contrasted with everyone you meet, see or know. It's based on fantasy, conjecture, and your own biases, but as you mature, you balance that with experience. You have the patterns of recent events and history as your metrics and you get to where the game becomes discerning between your desires and reality. War is a relentless and unforgiving teacher.”

dot’s single eye stare would not release Meghan’s attention. It was both using the skill dot had just described to X-ray Meghan as she turned the implications over in her head. Meghan stammered, “I mean, that all sounds…”

“Correct. Because you have had to learn it too.”

“Yes, but… not to that level, you’re predicting police tactics and how even…”

“…Prison guards are going to post that I’m here?”

“But you were the one who told them it would hurt their case.”

"Hackers call it social engineering."

"How could that help you?"

"Social engineering? Is it not obvious…"

"No, the guard… surely the protestors will only drive public opinion?"

"It's not the protestors."

"What, it's the guard?"

"Someone who would risk being fired is either a true believer, part of a bigger problem, or an entitled mutherfucker. I don't need either. A win either way."

"Something tells me, he's not a random casualty."

"And the light dawns."

Meghan pressed her, "Lemme guess, he's a chaser?"

"Unimportant. A pawn. Nothing more. In play…"

"But…"

"Shall we make the most of your time and get back to your agenda?"

Meghan's new found energy was instantly drained. dot could do that to ya, Like waking up the day after rolling and realizing that while you had been 'away', the world had indeed changed. Where had her epiphany's glow gone? She searched for the bright awareness that had carried her to here. She noted her notebook, checked her recorder.

"I would've reminded you if you hadn't been recording." Meghan shuddered like a dog shaking off the rain. She clung to the handrail of her mission to keep from fainting, "How did you get the bible to stick to the Pastor's chest?"

dot's eye receded into the gloom, "I painted it with a rubber cement and set it on fire, which seared it to his chest flesh. It smelled horrific and I almost hurled."

Meghan scribbled, "But the cement was not the accelerant you used."

"No, it was not. If the fire was too hot, it would've killed him too quickly, he would've just burned up before anyone got there. The bible was soaked in a precise measurement that would effectively remove his skin but not kill him right away, his nerves would be singed by the fire but not cauterized by it. It had to be precise to not cause so much pain that he died of it."

Meghan looked up, "So it was actually planned to the letter. Including who would show up and in what order?"

"Yes."

"You know I was the first on the scene."

"Yes. That's what scanners are for."

Meghan tried to hide the cold acid of adrenaline that just ripped through her body. She remembered that day. Until then, she had to rely on zoom interviews with the local spokespersons for her official statements, the one that happened in her own backyard seemed random… until now. Everything had seemed random, or self-determined, until now. She started to sweat and sat down.

"Are you all right, dear?"

"I'm just…" Meghan did feel faint. But Lucas' words the night before rang in her ears, "muhbee iz uh tess." And made her laugh. This was guts poker and Meghan was not going to fold, yet.

"Care to share?"

Meghan took a breath, "Not really… uh sorry," she shook it off and kept focus, "the eyes were a nice touch. Gruesome, but symbolic. Everything, The pyrotechnics, the first responders following protocols when they smelled the accelerant, and in so doing inadvertently allowing everyone to witness the Pastor's dying in agony… How did you know it would happen like that, and where did you learn all of this? How do you know so much about chemicals & fire?"

dot looked out blankly like a shark sensing chum in the water, "If you're asking if I have a military background, the answer is no. Yes it would've been a nice arrow in the ol' quiver, saving me weeks of YouTube research. But alas…"

"But come on, you're either a genius or you have better luck than anyone else in the world…"

"Meghan, dear, you know as well as I do, you make your own luck. And I would still like to know what just made you laugh."

Meghan flipped through her notebook, ignoring, "The precise page for the one biblical passage… Matthew 5:22, to send your message, survived a fire that completely eliminates the skin of an adult man. The eyes fell out of the sockets and stared only at the ground below. The news crew went live on Instagram just long enough to show the death, but could've been pulled back after the message was sent… it's a complicated string of events of which, everything has to go off without a moment's hesitation, and yet this…"

"Meghan honey, we were both there. Do you have a question in this?"

"Both there?"

"Who do you think lit the match?"

Meghan walked like a zombie to the cell door and stared in the window. dot was lying on her cot, her features obscured by the murky gloom, "You. Were. There. You lit the match and watched a man die a horrific death with the match still smoldering in your own hand."

"Well, you got a nice blockquote there, but remember he crawled out to meet you all, he lived for another 10 minutes or so before he finally succumbed."

"How…?"

"How. You're not asking how human life ends when the skin has been stripped away by fire. You're asking how can I do this. Again. And again. It's called life during wartime."

Meghan's knees wanted to buckle, but she did not want to succumb to dot's dark reality.

"I know this one was personal for you. But I'm assuming, that your editors are probably wanting more."

Meghan could feel her body calming down to a more flu-like soreness. She walked back to her notebook to catch her breath, "Do you have a lawyer, yet? Supposedly there's a court-appointed one…?"

"Meghan, are you listening to anything I've said? I can't ask anyone to sign-up for this. They will be getting death threats every day."

"Yes, but…"

"Besides, this is going to require body & soul commitment. I don't trust anyone to represent me with that."

"So, you're going to trust some court-appointed rando?"

"What would it matter? I'm not going to get a jury of my peers, either."

Meghan slumped into the cold steel chair that was bolted to the floor. She thumbed through her notes without seeing any words. She was losing the thread of her connection to the story and she knew it, “Can we get… personal?

“We can when you tell me what made you laugh.”

“Not going to happen. Deal breaker?”

dot pressed one eye against the window then pulled back into the gloom, “Deal breaker. Look who’s suddenly grown a backbone. No. No deal breaker.”

Meghan cleared her throat, “Our readers can get the details of your mission everywhere else. But I’m hoping to let them know who you are. I think we’ve covered why you’re doing it, so to speak.”

Both of dot’s eyes filled the window as if she was revealing them both together, “If you say so.”

Meghan locked eyes. For once, dot’s eyes were allowing Meghan in, rather than boring into her.

“When did you decide to go to war?”

“Actually, I had been contemplating it for many years, but after my spouse passed away, I had nothing else to live for, so the time had come.”

“Did your grief contribute to your decision?”

“Grief informs everything you do. It’s relentless. But, grief is debilitating, so… it’s not an asset, not a good companion in war.”

"Many have been speculating that you are funded by your own fortune, that you have a limitless source of money."

"Meghan, not many know I exist. If we're going to be honest with each other, it has to be complete and total. Please don't triangulate or use a fictitious "other" as a bank shot for your own thoughts or opinions."

"Fair. My apologies."

"If you weren't doing your own speculation, you wouldn't make a very professional reporter."

"Are you going to answer the question?"

"You know this answer. I've said it many times."

"That you can't ask anyone to join you in your mission?"

"Precisely."

"But you'd have to be extremely wealthy to afford just the travel alone."

"I did well before I went to war. But, I'm thrifty. It doesn't always take money. Sometimes, it's just a well-placed one or a zero."

"Fine. How did you pick your targets?"

"They picked themselves."

"That's vague. There's hundreds trying to kill us every day."

"Yes, but some are going to kill again. So, they can be stopped. At least from their next kill."

"Okay, well, that's still not an answer… but let's move on."

"Your call," replied dot from deep within her cell.

Meghan saw that dot had indeed left her window, "What did you mean last night when you said that it wasn't the end of the mission."

Meghan's question was echoing off the walls when she realized it was the first time that dot didn't have an immediate answer. It was another two breaths before she heard dot seem to clear her throat.

"Do you feel like you have enough of who I am to be switching gears?"

"I can think nonlinearly."

"And so you think I can too. Interesting."

"You can't? I find that extremely hard to believe."

"I didn't say I couldn't, I just find your assumption… interesting."

"Isn't that what you do? Assume behavior and exploit it?"

"Wow. That's a bold leap. Careful, you don't want to pull something."

"I've noticed you use snark to cover or maybe buy time."

"I use snark to remind someone where the guard rails are. The least dangerous person is the one who thinks they know everything."

Meghan stopped and took a breath.

"You'll be hearing how the ones who abused Kel on the Pastor's behalf… won't be graduating from high school."

Meghan tried to process, "Because they'll be dead?"

"Kel was robbed of all that life had to offer, especially, and you know this, someone who had found their true and genuine self— call me old fashioned, but I just don't like that word authentic. Kel was a very happy kid, these fuckers destroyed that, and never gave it a second thought, so… they will have some fleeting moments to find second and third thoughts, if they are capable of self-reflection, which… it's even odds now that they aren't."

"But… don't you think that I now have an obligation to warn them?"

"I suppose you could try. That's why I asked when your article was going to post."

"I suppose, hopefully before your trial begins… and people know why they should care… and the press embargo is lifted?"

"That makes sense. How would you warn them? And what would you say is coming? And how would you tell them about me without telling them about me or why you have this information?"

Meghan set her notebook down and turned off her recorder.

"War teaches you to think in four dimensions."

"There's three."

"The fourth is time."

"Fuck."

She peered into the gloom of dot's cell door window. The grime made it even more reflective and Meghan could see only herself in the small rectangle surrounded by steel. She was small. Lost. Contained.

Meghan closed her notebook, "I won't be here tomorrow, I'll be showing my progress outline to my editor to decide if I get to go on."

"Good luck."

"I thought we make our own luck."

Meghan stood and packed her things, silently and waited for the door to the anti-cell to open.

5

"

the snake never stops eating its own tail.

"

Meghan opened the door to their apartment to see that dinner had been left for her. A candle had burned down to a nub and the half bottle of wine had, she would soon know, finally opened up. She looked to the couch to see that Lucas had fallen asleep with the vintage Nintendo controller still in their hands; the high game entry page still on the screen. Meghan shook her head, grabbed the cold but still delicious cauliflower "hot wing," dragged it through the ranch sauce, grabbed the bottle, and headed for Lucas' arms. She popped the breaded treat into her mouth smearing the ranch sauce on her cheek, and washed it down with a huge swig from the bottle.

Lucas opened their eyes and smiled at the squirrel cheek-stuffed face that was happily sucking on the bottle of wine. They wiped half the ranch sauce from her cheek and wiped it on the other cheek and striped the nose to complete the effect. Meghan and Lucas kissed long with Meghan chewing between each one to finish dinner so she could enjoy her lover. One last slug of wine and she was finally ready to talk. Lucas grabbed the bottle and took a swig, "So… you know that dude that was caught on camera knocking down the Pride mannikins in that Target in Arizona… *on Grindr.*"

Meghan took the bottle back, "So predictable. Thanks for the wings. Very sweet." Lucas pulled her closer, "knew you'd be hangry. How'd it go?" Meghan took another pull from the bottle, swallowed, and handed it back, "I think I got enough for my meeting with Jan tomorrow. Bitch's in my head, though."

Lucas sipped, "Jan?" and took another sip and saw that there was only one left, and handed it to Meghan. She kissed their cheek and finished the bottle, "Jan's always in my head, I meant dot."

"But what's their real name?"

Meghan stopped and realized, nobody had talked about this yet, "I… haven't asked yet? That's fucking weird. They're in a state Penitentiary for fuck's sake, they just always lead me up the stairs and then let me out… Meghan slumped further into Lucas' arms, "She's fucking right. I… don't think in four dimensions…"

Lucas leaned forward and opened the wooden stash box on the coffee table, “Aren’t there three?” Meghan shook her head, “The fourth is time.” Lucas took out a preroll, lit up, and handed it to Meghan, she took a hit and handed it back, “There’s protests outside the Pen’s entrance. Somebody broke the embargo.”

Lucas hit it and handed it back, but Meghan waved them off, “No more, I’ve got to get up early for Jan.” Meghan rolled onto Lucas’ lap and took off their shirt, revealing a large tattoo of a wolf on their chest. Meghan ran her hands over their chest, caressed the scars that the tattoo’s job was to hide, kissed the scars, and kept on kissing right up their neck onto their face. Lucas deftly unbuttoned Meghan’s pants and pulled them down so she could writhe out of them. Lucas reached between her legs and caressed her gently yet confidently, then licked their hand and found gold. Meghan practically collapsed onto their chest in joy and within minutes was chewing on Lucas’s ear in ecstasy.

“Hey. Baby. It’s time.”

Meghan shook off disorientation – she was safe. She was in Lucas’s arms. But they weren’t on the couch and it wasn’t night…

… Anymore. Meghan’s alarm was still chirping and Lucas was standing over her with coffee. She sat up, and took the coffee, “What would I do without you?” Lucas grinned and hugged her to standing, “Neither of us wants to find out.” They lead her to the bathroom where the shower was already running. “You are too good to me.”

"I am too good *for* you. That's why you are lucky beyond words." Meghan handed her coffee to Lucas and stepped into the hot spray – perfect temperature. "You are the most perfect lover." She said as the water warmed her body. She pulled the curtain to find them waiting for her, a quick kiss pushed her back into the task at hand.

Jan Henderson had been in publishing since before Meghan had been born. She'd ridden the wave from print to electronic with grace because, to her, they weren't different, which was contrary to her mostly male counterparts who thought if they resisted change they could stop it. Jan considered the new platforms as merely new tools of the trade.

Jan made it her business to get it. All of it. She understood the metrics (or rather she made it look like she did, when in truth, it was the product of spending her nights studying when the boys were in the clubs lamenting the death of the business as they had known it). Story was story. News was news. It was still who, what, where, when, & how despite what any algorithms promised, or AI threatened.

Meghan loved working for Jan and learned something every time she spoke with her. But she was intimidated by her, and of course, never really felt prepared.

But at least she was caffeinated, thanks to Lucas. She watched as Jan read her outline, trying to discern from her eye movement and facial expressions where she could be.

This is how these things went. Jan didn't give a rip how you felt about your material, it was how it read. If fact, it was better for you if you weren't in the room. Even though this was just the outline stage, Meghan was expected to have her 'voice shining through,' 'the direction fleshed out' and 'the destination needed to be more than hinted at.' Lucas was also right, Jan was all the way up in Meghan's head.

Jan finished and turned her chair to face away from Meghan. She ran her fingers through her hair and exhaled, took off her glasses, rubbed her eyes, composed herself then turned back to face Meghan, "She's holding nothing back and she's not looking for mercy. But, something's brewing. I just don't know what it is."

Meghan hid her smile, Jan was as invested as she was and she was coming to this from Meghan's pages. Meghan stared at Jan. "I… she, dot, may have slipped, and I think some more people are going to be hurt. I think she put some… thing in place that may happen automatically?"

Jan rubbed her eyes, "How would you let them know, without breaking the embargo?"

"Maybe tell the warden at the Pen."

"Oh sweetheart, they already know everything you two have said."

Meghan felt like she got kicked in the stomach. Of course, she thought, they had to be listening. They needed anything they could get to put dot away, "They don't have anything on her, do they?"

Jan smiled sadly, “Let’s just say that if they hadn’t already gotten a confession, they wouldn’t have anything. They don’t even know her real name.”

“It’s true, then,” Meghan felt the room start to spin. She was in the center of the breaking down of reality. If dot hadn’t come forward, she would still be out there effectively at war. “They didn’t know who she was,” said Meghan, “and the protestors are so fucking dumb that they don’t even know that all of what she’s confessed to is connected. How the fuck, can they not know her name?”

Jan shook her head, “She… doesn’t exist. No record. No… nothing. She’s a ghost. Even the CIA has no idea who she is, or where she came from. She has no connection anywhere, no family. No past. No… anything. Except… you.”

Meghan stood and started pacing, “She could actually get off of this thing.” Jan joined her in her pacing, “Would that be a good thing?” Meghan stopped, “She said she’s on a mission, but realized that she could never kill ‘em all… what makes me pause is… what happens when you can’t fulfill your mission?”

Jan slumped into her chair, “Give up?”

“dot’s not a quitter.”

“Then why did she turn herself in?”

Meghan found herself parroting dot’s explanation, “This is supposed to be some sort of a reset…?”

"What's that supposed to mean?"

"Well, until now I thought I understood… but, I guess I thought she intended for our article to get her story out there?"

"I'm not buying it. She's too far in to fail." Jan fumbled for her glasses, realized they were on her head, and put them on, "She must think she's going to make them look foolish putting her on trial. Destroy their credibility?"

Meghan shook her head, "To what end? All of her other victims have actual blood on their hands. What has the state government or attorney General done?"

"I can dig, maybe we missed something?" Jan sat at her computer and started typing into her search engine.

Meghan looked over Jan's shoulder, "I dunno… I… suppose she'll tell me…"

Jan and Meghan finished the sentence together "When she wants us to know."

Meghan sat in her chair, "She keeps asking when we're going to post the story."

Jan threw her glasses onto her desk. "I've got a bad feeling. She isn't planning on going to trial."

Meghan shook her head trying to clear it, "That's why she's telling me everything. Are we seriously just waiting for the embargo to lift after jury selection?"

Jan rubbed her eyes, “And your finished piece goes through proof and legal. So, do your part and color within the lines. I know this one is personal for you…”

Meghan frowned, “Oh, because I’m the Trans whisperer.”

Jan stood and showed Meghan the door, “No. Because you were the first one on scene at the barn. And she… chose you. Now, get to work and bring this one home.”

Lucas was waiting in the lobby, dressed for a date. Meghan stepped off the elevator and walked up behind them. Wrapping her arms around them, she purred, “I’m starved and I need a drink.” Lucas turned in her arms and kissed her hello. Several writers from the site walked past and waved goodnight to Meghan. She sheepishly waved back, Lucas kissed her again while proudly waving, “Well, it seems we’re celebrating, so… I’ve got the perfect place.”

“Where would we have gone if it hadn’t gone well?” Lucas led her to the exit, “Straight to a bar that makes stiffies.” Meghan laughed, “You, of all people know…I don’t do anything straight.”

“I’m wondering if that line will ever get funny,” queried Lucas as they held the door for Meghan. “Hey,” she bit their nose as she stepped past, “You’re not the only one who gets to do Dad jokes.”

As they jumped up into Lucas’ truck, Meghan was a little ‘homesick’ for the Pen and her conversations with dot. It felt weird to have a night off and was always weird when she felt attached to someplace as depressing as a prison, and someone as dangerous as dot.

Lucas, on the other hand, was in seventh heaven ~ they were at their best when they got to spoil their girl. All Lucas ever needed was half an excuse to turn the fun light on. They pulled into the public lot and started across the street to Spirit Elephant. Meghan knew that as much as Lucas loved their meat, when they picked a vegan restaurant, it was a real date. The hostess smiled as she asked if they had reservations, and Meghan was about to answer when Lucas confidently said, "Rojas for 2 at 6:00 pm."

The hostess led them as they serpentined through the already crowded restaurant, weaving in and out of the tables, Meghan asked over her shoulder, "So… how did you know it was going to go this well?" Lucas grinned triumphantly, "Come on, when you jumped up from your third orgasm and immediately started typing your article, I knew it was going to be great."

"Lucas!" Meghan hissed while trying to turn invisible and follow the hostess simultaneously, "Stop bragging in public." Lucas acknowledged the stares as they passed the bar, "Where else do you do it?" The widescreen over the bar displayed the news of a man's murder, but the sound was turned off. It was the caption that caught Meghan's eye. She stopped to read: Trans Teen's Tormentor Burned Alive. The Hostess backtracked to Meghan, "Oh, yeah, that piece of shit thought he was getting away with it so, he went after another high schooler. Serves him right."

The Hostess smiled patiently, and waited until they began to follow her again, "How did he die?" asked Lucas, as he danced between the chairs and coats hanging off them. Meghan slid through the crowd stepping up to the Hostess, "They're not sure, but there was a bible in his hands that had been soaked in some sort of chemical…" Lucas, slid beside her, and held the chair for Meghan as the Hostess handed them menus, "Posie will be your server, enjoy," and left. Meghan stared at Lucas, "I may have lost my appetite. I'm sorry?"

Lucas reached across and cupped her hands with their own, "There's always alcohol."

The server took their orders for Lavender Gimlets, and Meghan pulled out her phone, "I know I'm breaking our rule, but…" and scrolled through the news feeds, "These are the assholes who worked with Pastor…"

Lucas nodded their head, "Yeah, yeah, Barbie Cue, Al Pastor, I know."

Meghan winced, "That's so gross."

The server set their drinks down, "Do you need a minute still to order dinner?" Lucas handed Meghan her drink and shrugged to the server, who nodded and left. They toasted as Meghan read aloud, "The bible was mostly burned in the blaze that had leveled the house, but was opened to Matthew 5:22. Shit! That's the same one used for the Pastor. no other people or structures were damaged. Fuck. So, either dot's getting lazy or she's making sure we connect this guy to the Pastor. Or… since she's in custody, maybe making it look like a copycat?"

Lucas drained their cocktail, "what about the notebook paper with the three dots?" Meghan made sure no one was in earshot, "We're the only ones who know about those. The FBI doesn't want that to get out."

Lucas caught the server's eye and waved their empty glass, "Are they afraid it will catch on?" Meghan sipped her cocktail, "No, they use details like that to establish the connection for real suspects." Lucas shrugged, "Makes sense. So what does this mean?" Meghan reached across and cupped Lucas' hands, "It means… I'm not hungry, babe. Can we go after your next cocktail? I mean… we still have that posole from your mom and I…"

Lucas tilted their chair back, "How bout you at least get something to go? I really wanted you to try this place out?"

Meghan nodded, "it's was the least I can do, for my Luscious Lucius."

They spent the rest of the night scouring the internet for news and details of the new murder. The consensus seemed to be that they were connected only by their association and similarities but not one article mentioned if the same suspect had committed both crimes, only that police did not have a suspect in the new murders, and not one mention of dot's calling card, the note with the three connected dots had been left behind.

Meghan had argued that that was a police technique to prey on the ego of the killer who would be mad that they weren't getting the credit for their work. Lucas thought it was because even though the police were playing dumb, they knew that dot had confessed to the Pastor's murder when she turned herself in.

Whatever the reason, if Jan was right and the Pen's warden was listening in on their conversation, then by now, they would know that dot had been warning them, and the window was closing for her to take care of Kel's remaining two bullies. Unless, of course, that had been dot's plan all along. It made Meghan want to scream that dot had conditioned her to doubt her doubts… the snake never stopped eating its own tail.

But at least it kick-started her delivery draft of the article. She'd blazed a reasonably readable version to date, now it just remained to be seen what dot's next move would be.

And that would be a tomorrow thing.

6

"

…who the fuck knows in this palace of mirrors?

"

Meghan considered entering through the main entrance of the Pen but pulled up at the last minute. The last thing she needed was to have her face associated with a bunch of toothless rednecks protesting a woman they didn't know and an issue they could never hope to understand.

She went through processing without a hitch or incident, neither she nor the clerk were very talkative today, and her escort was their usually silent, gruff self. It was a day like any other one of this assignment until she got into dot's anti-cell…

“Hello, Ms. Woods,” said the athletic and scrubbed white woman in her thirties, “I’m Officer Taylor, and I’ll be observing from now on.”

“We’re on suicide watch, Megs, apparently I said something to you the other day that triggered the lifeguards.”

Meghan took Officer Taylor’s hand, shook it once, and then looked to the cell window. The light was on inside dot’s cell and Meghan could see just how small it was. dot was a tiny figure lying on her cot, staring at the ceiling. She was frailer than Meghan had imagined, but the scratched and grimy glass still blurred her features and Meghan could only tell that her buzz cut was just barely starting to grow out. dot appeared every bit of sixty that she had claimed to be.

As Meghan pulled her recorder & notebook from her backpack, she nodded to Officer Taylor, “So… how’s this going to work?”

dot answered from the cell, “Don’t mind her, she’ll be as quiet as a church mouse, nothing she hears would be admissible, anyway. We’ve still got our mission. Steady as she goes.”

Officer Taylor nodded and smiled as dot continued, “Besides, she’s our sister, how she ever got into the academy in this climate is anybody’s guess.” Officer Taylor’s face was a mask of practiced poker calm. Meghan couldn’t quite tell if dot just figured that out or already knew, so she gave her sister the grace of space, which *was* the tell now for both women. A cis person would either crave inclusion, even if it was only tangential, and begin “the interview” or immediately try to repel any suspicion, with cringy apologies. Either way it would be crowded with a cis person's sense of self suddenly taking it's half out of the middle.

Meghan did wonder who set-up who, as she clocked herself being one of three trans women together in this cold maximum-security prison on this day… if Officer Taylor clocked it as well, Meghan would only get the slightest shallowing of her breath as everyone but dot checked and doubled checked the exits. "Yep, we're everywhere," sighed dot as Officer Taylor took a seat in the corner to allow Meghan to get to work,

Meghan started the recording, "You know they still don't know your name. And it was a little embarrassing when I had to confess to my editor that I didn't either."

dot rolled away from the window to stare into her wall, "So it went well, then? Your editor has been paying attention, and we're all on track."

Meghan shook her head, "No notes, just some requests that will make it more of a feature article. Like a name, maybe a more fleshed out personal history, you know, the usual…"

"I'm actually growing fond of the name, dot. As for the backstory, well ask away. I'm an open book, ain't that right, Officer Taylor?"

Officer Taylor's blank face and red hair seemed to absorb the jab, but Meghan jotted the note and cleared her throat, "Speaking of books… one got delivered in Ohio last night."

"You mean yesterday. They don't deliver at night unless it's at

Christmas time."

"You're not even the slightest bit… it's going to seem like quite the feat to have been accomplished while being in custody, nice touch. But what if they attribute it to a copycat?"

"I will need a little bit more info to understand what you're talking about."

Meghan sat on the table so she could peer through the window better, "Oh, so what happened to that open book?"

"I'm waiting to know what could be attributed to a copycat."

Officer Taylor flinched as the alert sounded from her phone. She pulled it out as a video started playing, "Another murder in Ohio…" before she could stop it and sheepishly jam it back into her pocket. Meghan stared at Officer Taylor, who nodded discretely and looked away.

"So… there's that. Care to comment?"

"Meghan, you seem to be asking me to read your mind today."

"My apologies. It seems there were additional murders that were connected to the Pastor from Ohio. I don't have all of the details, but it looks very much like the work you've confessed to. Since you've been in State custody for weeks now, it would appear impossible that you are responsible. One could surmise that you are not who you say you are, that is, responsible for any of these murders, and that in actual fact, the killer is still at large. What would you say to that?"

dot was staring out the window – her eyes filling the small rectangle, "That's my girl."

Meghan walked closer to the cell door. They locked eyes and dot's eyes smiled, "I suppose I have no control over what people think. If you're asking me to comment about three people…"

"Three?" Meghan glanced to Officer Taylor, whose face was frozen in neutrality, neither confirming nor denying, which of course meant it was true.

"… who got what they deserved, albeit a bit later than planned, or maybe then they expected, I'd say, 'Gosh, isn't that interesting.' But if you're asking how the congregation who willfully exploited and exacerbated a child's fears and vulnerability for nothing other than a contest of cruelty will deal with this? Well then, they now know there's nowhere to hide and hopefully, they will live in the fear of their own eventual coming retribution."

Meghan opened her mouth to speak, but no words came. She kept waiting for dot to move, say something, or do anything that would dispel the chill that frosted the cell.

When none came, she retreated to the comfort of her notebook, like a life raft adrift in the arctic sea of dot's resolve. She noted the counter on her recorder in her notebook. Professionalism, the only handrail in her life raft, "So… so… it was a fear tactic?"

"Kel was a bag of fear the last days of his young life. The entire congregation, and, a quick aside, his parents were the ones who poked that bear first, outing their own child to their youth minister so, they are not blameless, and they've paid their price. But everyone *else* in that 'church' shoulders the blame. They supported Kel's persecution. They 'prayed for it'. Who the fuck prays for harm to come to anyone? These people do. These stunted humans are masters at rationalizing their actions into abstractions for easy disposal.

If you wait long enough, their denial and mental calisthenics eventually stop working, and they as people simply… break, they cease being effective in the world and at least they stop hurting themselves and others."

"So… I gotta ask, why not just wait."

"Because between now and then, if they think they've gotta away with it – they do it again, and another Kel dies. So before that ever happens again, they will feel their own fears claw away their mental health from the inside, just like Kel."

"And what if it just inspires them to hurt more of us? These are the fuckers who've waged war in their God's name for centuries."

"No, these are the last dregs of that gene pool. They get distracted by the next shiny object. If they didn't have the goad to their flanks by the actuaries that fleece them with the next cultural outrage, they wouldn't know what to do with their lives. They've been promised a return to some version of life where they are still the top of the heap. That's not coming, ever. But hope is very powerful even if it's for a cruel outcome, and so… hope is next."

"You're particularly cynical, today. And you're sounding a little like a conspiracy theorist."

dot laughed for the first time in two weeks. It caught both Meghan and Officer Taylor off guard.

dot stood from her cot and walked to her toilet and sat to pee. Meghan looked away from the cell door to give her a modicum of privacy, turned off the recorder, and waited until the flush subsided. Meghan watched as dot shuffled back to her cot, before resuming the recording, "Did you know you were going to time the two, sorry three murders yesterday with when you would be in lock-up? Or was that already in motion when you decided to turn yourself in?"

"Are you looking for an exclusive or a confession?"

Meghan nodded to Officer Taylor, "But, you are… you did…" Meghan checked her notes, "That's… sorry, you haven't taken credit or responsibility for their deaths. I… it's been assumed by your responses…. Yes. I see that now."

"I set it in motion before I turned myself in. They need to be constantly looking over their shoulder. Ironically, and yet expected, they have not increased any safety precautions at the church. Which… will have proved to be unfortunate."

Meghan scribbled in her notebook, "You are using a disproportionate amount of energy against this church, compared to the other killings, I know I asked you this before, but… is this one personal?"

Meghan hadn't noticed that dot was staring at her from the window, with one single eye, unblinking, "Meghan. If you going to dissect my tactics and motivation, don't mistake long-term strategy for an emotional response. These smaller groups of humans are the ones who do the harshest damage to real people. Kel was a real child. He was not the faceless enemy that these people have been indoctrinated to hate from afar. He was a child, their child, a child of that village, and yet they acted on their cruelest impulses. There are hundreds of Kels and hundreds of congregations across this country. I can't be everywhere at once, but I can put the next one on notice."

dot stepped back from the window and turned her back. She seemed fatigued. Shoulders slumped, head bowed. Meghan realized she hadn't taken a breath for some time, so she inhaled, "Can we go back to before this all started? You must've had a life. You must've had…. different plans?"

"A future. Yes. I had the standard happily ever after until she died. Then, I thought I was supposed to find love again. But then the war became so… blatant. And, since I didn't have an attachment to another heart, yet, I realized that this was by design."

"Design. You mean… divinely inspired?"

"Reporters like to sound like they're paying attention by pouncing on what they think are incongruences."

"Yes, far be it from you to blame your actions on some God or do anything in the name of one."

"The most dangerous woman is the one with nothing to lose. So. Whatever had been on the ol' to-do list, was backburnered. And war became… me."

"But you haven't answered my question."

"You are right. It's like your life before transition. There were good times and bad, but it's all enshrouded in dysphoria's murky fog. When we're lucky, that's all that remains, yes? It's of no interest to me, with the exception being that I know at one time it had been all I had. But for your article, I had been married for almost 30 years, and I had been in computers. I got good at them, then I started to be fascinated by the lengths some went to protect them, so I got good at that too, and bang, zoom pretty soon, I had my own security consulting firm."

"Having a marriage and your own business should've put you into the system, how come they're having such a hard time finding out even simple things like your name?"

dot turned and walked back to the door and pressed her face to the window, both eyes were all that were visible. She stared unblinking, her eyes seemed to be patiently smiling. Meghan met her gaze, and then it dawned.

"Fuck," said Meghan, "Ok… so… fuck, so that's how you know who's doing the worst deeds as well?"

"Well, no. If I just relied on the web, I'd only know about pain & suffering after the fact. And people, especially the police are notorious for keeping shitty records when it comes to our community, they don't usually document their cruelty. The mission is for the Kels of the world to grow old and die from natural causes after long and fruitful lives."

"So… then… what happens to your mission when you're convicted of multiple murders and in prison for life or… well, you've committed at least six of your murders in states where you face the death penalty. So, what happens then?"

"We've been over this before. Do you want to check your notes?"

"I'm not talking about your motivations here, I'm asking strategically, you have… thought this through, right? So… ?"

"The scales will be balanced. That's all I can hope for. What happens after that is none of my business."

Meghan slumped into her chair as if she'd been suddenly dropped there. "I wasn't able to find if you'd left your calling card at yesterday's Ohio murders."

"The Feddy's got the press trained up well."

"So it was there."

"Is that a question, Meghan?"

"I guess, I'm asking for you to confirm if it's true."

"Well, since I wasn't there, I can't confirm anything, can I?"

"But… you are responsible for yesterday's murders in Ohio?"

"I take full responsibility."

Meghan started to speak. A full confession to a crime that hadn't been charged to dot was the last thing she ever expected to hear. It felt like lightning had struck the room. What more could Meghan ask or say? Even getting dot to confirm she'd left a calling card seemed moot. Meghan reached forward and stopped the recorder.

She stared at the cell door then quietly packed up her things and sat for a moment with her backpack on her lap, staring at the floor.

She stood without looking at Officer Taylor and walked to the door. It shrieked its electrical scowl as the bolt snapped open, the door protesting once again that it was opening. Meghan waited until the sound merely echoed into the cavernous Pen, and then whisper over her shoulder, "Well, thanks…" and stepped out of the cell.

The door cried aloud as she walked the catwalk, and its slamming echoed behind her.

As soon as Meghan's cellphone was handed back to her, she fired it up to search the news – notification after notification rammed onto her screen as soon as she got service.

The Night Clerk, a no-nonsense Black woman with hair pulled into a tight bun, raised an eyebrow at the sound of so many alerts, "Seems someone was missed like hell." Meghan shrugged politely and pulled up her collar of her coat against the spring chill. She jammed the phone into her pocket and hurried out the door. Lucas was waiting for her, “I know you’re an independent woman and all…” Meghan shut them up by planting a huge kiss on their lips, then jumped into the truck before Lucas even knew what hit them.

She pulled out her phone and scrolled through forty or so breaking news alerts pouring in from Ohio. Lucas jumped in and stared at her with an amused grin on their face, waiting for Meghan to look up. She read the account of the double murder from this morning that had resulted in a church fire, reading out loud, “burning the chapel to the ground. Fuck. King. A…”

She stare at Lucas, turning her phone for them to see. Lucas read the headline, “Oh shit. Your life just got way more interesting. Hungry?” Meghan suddenly realized she was. And faint. And little sick to her stomach. All at once. She nodded meekly. Lucas raised a bag of to-go food marked “Planet Plant,” the aroma of the Impossible Burger and fries finally getting into her senses, She wrapped her arms around Lucas with abandon and snatched the bag from them hungrily, “What the actual fuck would I do without you?”

Lucas started the truck and put it into gear, “We’ve been through this, but the general consensus is even money on 'whither and die'.” Meghan dug into the bag, “And a Chocolate Almond-butter shake? Marry me?” Lucas steered out onto the interstate, “Nah, too patriarchal. How bout, commit to you forever, verbally?”

Meghan took a huge bite from the burger and a pull from the shake, “Romantic, AF.”

Meghan happily chewed and slurped as she scowled through the news feeds, it was horrendous. The tone of the reports had pulled a 180 from the day before, speculation of the connection to both incidents was now being connected to the Pastors' demise and hinted at an even larger conspiracy, but both the FBI and IBI & Ohio State Police were vague about suspects, which of course had set the right-wing social media on fire. The account from the AP was so far, the most reliable, even though the report was rife with bias, it still provided a first-person account of the crime scene, one that would be both 'watered-up' as dot had said and watered down with the various retellings by both bot and human.

"Three companies of firefighters responded to a blaze at the Christ the Redeemer, United Church of Christ congregation this morning. Fire Captain, John T. Campion announced via press conference that the blaze had ignited at 10:17 am this morning, when two separate packages containing bibles were opened simultaneously mixing two chemicals in an industrial accelerant commonly used in the construction industry. There were two fatalities, James Martin (20) and Ronald Dalton (19) who were believed to have been the ones to whom the packages were addressed, and were later confirmed via Postal Archive and dental records."

Meghan shook her head, "dot doesn't miss a trick." Lucas stared ahead, finally happy to hear Meghan's voice, "So, who were these two, how were they connected, again?"

Meghan finished the last of her fries and folded the top down on the bag to stash at her feet, "Remember that victim that I was reading to you at Spirit Elephant? Well, there were three men who helped that Pastor inflict conversion therapy on Kel. These were the other two."

Lucas nodded, "Yeah. Sounds like they got what they deserved."

Meghan stared out the window into the dark, "Well, yes. They were each found charred into unrecognizable piles, the bibles were seared onto their hands, so they probably weren't able to let go of them once they ignited…"

"What the… how the fuck does she… even think that shit up?" gasped Lucas, "I mean, that's next-level shit."

Meghan softly put her head against the window, hoping the vibration would wake her from this fevered dream, "I'm trying to figure out how dot would know that they would be together at the church, and why were they even at the church on a weekday morning? It's like she's… And how do you plan this far in advance? Like so many variables have to fall into place perfectly. I just don't understand."

They drove in silence for the last miles of the Interstate before Lucas broke the quiet, "I still can't tell if this is going to hurt our community or help us." Meghan didn't answer until they turned into their neighborhood, "It doesn't matter to her. She's probably not planning on being with us too much longer."

Lucas pulled to a stop, "You think she'll get the death penalty?" Meghan turned to Lucas, a flood of mixed feelings sweeping across her face, "I... think I was wrong about her. I don't think she's planning on standing trial."

Lucas inched forward to an open slot on the street. And parked. They got out and trudged up the stairs to their apartment.

Meghan thought she was tired, but as soon as her teeth were brushed and her pajamas on, she grabbed her laptop and headed for bed. Lucas was way ahead of her, laptop on their knees, rabbitholing on the web. Meghan cocked her head then snuggled in beside them and looked over their shoulder at their screen. Lucas was in deep, "The 4 chans and telegraphs of the world are trumpeting this as an LGBTQ+ conspiracy, but none of them are using the word, Trans. So, they don't know that dot is Trans, do they?"

Meghan opened her laptop, "No one did. Until she turned herself in, they hadn't a clue, and they still don't even with her in custody. The moron guard that posted that they had the Pastor Killer in custody, didn't know her identity or even all the murders she confessed to. The protestors only know her as The Anti-Christ."

Lucas took off their reading glasses and rubbed their eyes, "Wouldn't that make the Pastor, Jesus?"

Meghan didn't even look up, "This is what's frustrating her, connecting the dots is never their strong suit. But it is interesting that without any facts, the stormcrows know at least *why* they may have been murdered. Either someone on the inside is leaking or…"

"Or they believe someone *should* be coming for them."

Meghan hit play on a newsfeed video showing a sobbing woman

being interviewed in front of the smoldering ruins of the church, behind her, firefighters were taking care of the last of the hotspots. "My James met Ronald to help out our temporary pastor." The reporter's voice continued as ruins and a small ragged group identified as members of the congregation were shown, "The temporary pastor was fortunately offsite running errands when the fire started."

A scared-looking man in his mid-forties appeared on Meghan's screen, a graphic identified him as Pastor Michael Smith, Temporary Pastor, "I wasn't gone that long, I didn't even know James & Ronald were here."

Meghan selected a different tab on her search engine and came across a shot of two cellphones with a graphic that posted in bold across the screen, GAY HOOKUP IS FIRE! Meghan enlarged the screenshot of a cellphone screen to read:

"BJ? BASEMENT JOB?"

"FUCKING TEASE."

"SERIOUSLY GIRL MEET ME BEFORE YOU GO TO SCHOOL AND I'LL ROCK YOUR WORLD!"

"YASSSS"

The messages were dated this morning at 7:00 am.

Meghan turned her screen for Lucas to read, she pointed to the text messages. They stared, reading, and then shook their head,

“Cliche’d as fuck.” Meghan turned her screen back, “But that’s some serious leakage… we have to have one of our siblings on the inside.” Lucas snapped their computer closed and turned out the light on their nightstand, “Or an ally.” Meghan was typing furiously, “I suppose that’s also a possibility. Who the fuck knows in this palace of mirrors?”

Lucas kissed her on the cheek and rolled over to sleep, “I suppose either is a comforting thought.” Meghan kept typing for another four pages before yawning as the adrenaline that had been keeping her aloft for the past two hours evaporated under her wings. She closed the laptop and snuggled into Lucas’ embrace.

7

"

Ten minutes of that will get you back into the right side of your day.

"

The loud knocking woke Meghan but Lucas was still dead to the world. She grabbed her bathrobe as she headed for the door, "Hold on… Who is it?"

"FBI ma'am."

Meghan stopped and peered out the peephole. Two suit-clad men stood holding their badges for her to see. She fixed her hair and unbolted the door, "Um, good morning?"

“Ms. Woods, we’d like to talk to you about federal inmate number W10042574.” Meghan leaned against the doorjamb, “Awe Agent…?”

“Smith.”

“Agent Smith. You’re not making this up are you?” The Agent stared at her stoically as if trying to will his face into a smile but was only able to accomplish its default, professional neutrality mode, “No ma’am.”

“Ah, well then, Agent Smith, you know that it is highly inappropriate for you to come to my home. If you have questions, it's best to go through the legal department at Kincaid Publishing…”

“It’s believed that you are in danger. We’ve been assigned as your protection, ma’am.” Meghan bit her lip, “S’cuse me?”

“May we come in?” Meghan’s “No,” came out almost involuntarily. “I’m sorry, but we’re still sleeping? Can’t you protect me from outside? Wouldn’t any threat be trying to come through this door?”

The Agents looked to each other, clearly, that wasn’t an option they appreciated. Meghan took their hesitation as her “Yes” and nodded, “Excellent. Thank you. Let me know If you need anything else.” And shut the door. Agent Smith put up his hand to stop the door, but the other Agent stopped him and whispered something in his ear. Meghan watched from the peephole as they both stared into it knowing she was likely there. They turned and settled in to stand guard.

Meghan practically ran back to the bedroom and Lucas' arms. She grabbed her cell phone and hit a speed dial as she answered Lucas' questioning yawn, "FBI. They're here to protect us. Hi Jan, sorry, I know it's…" she checked her phone, "6:10? Shit, sorry. The FBI is guarding my door…"

"Guarding…? Did you call them?"

"No. There's two of them. So, you didn't know about this?"

"Hang on…"

Meghan heard the line go silent, then, she heard Jan's voice again and a ringing, "I'm getting legal on the line."

"Jeezus Jan, it's… 6:11? Are you okay?"

"Hi, Abby. I've got Meghan Woods on the line she's just been awakened by the FBI, saying two agents had been sent to protect her. She's on the Trans Serial Killer currently in custody at the Pen."

"Well, I wouldn't say she's a serial killer, and I never said she was Trans…"

"Honey, Abby only knows things by their slugs. Abby, do you know anything about this?"

"Good morning Meghan, no Jan."

"Abby, what should she do? She's got two more days of interviewing before the trial."

"Okay Ladies, let's just relax and let me make some calls. Meghan are you all right?"

Jan cut her off before she could speak, "Abby, why should she, a Black Trans woman allow two FBI Agents into the home that she shares with a Latino Non-Binary lover? What could possibly go wrong?"

"Well, Jan… Meghan now that I know more about you than HR is probably comfortable with, let's just not poke any bears and wait for my call. Cool?"

Meghan spoke before Jan could answer for her. "I'm cool with that."

"Thanks, Meghan, and thank you Jan. Bye now."

"Meghan, you all right?"

"Yes, Jan, I'm fine. Thank you."

Meghan hung up and rolled into Lucas' arms once again.

Meghan sat in the back of the SUV as it passed the EL stop where she ordinarily would be switching to the ride service du jour to get to the Pen. The Protection detail was legit, Abby had determined, and, being practical, negotiated them driving Meghan to work every day going forward to appease all. Except Meghan. It took everything she had to not jump out of the moving vehicle. She drilled harder into her article using the time to study her two personal Agents to include them in the article.

They were as tightlipped as could be expected, but they did let on that it was after the events in Ohio that precipitated the need. "If it helps, we've also got a detail on all of the members of the media that were there when the Pastor was murdered."

It didn't. Help that is. But in the fog of the of her new normal of waking - EL - then Lyft (now Protection Detail's SUV) - Pen-sign in- Gruffy escort - dot (and now Officer Taylor) gobsmacking by dot - home - (either by Trusty Truck in Lucas's arm or now, Protection Detail) wine - both Lucas's arms (and the lips, chin, hair etc. that comes with) - Lucas's cooking (on the better nights) - more wine - writing, dot's gobsmacking all over again - more wine - sleep (if that's what you call it) shower-rinse- repeat (all usually with Lucas's help, cheerleading, or down right doing it to her themself)…

… she had only now thought about her fellow "culties"…

Letting the wave of guilt and self-criticism (which five years of therapy had elevated from loathing) she wondered if they had protection details, were they okay? What they might think… now? And when it might be appropriate to message them… and why none of them had messaged her…

Her stomach suddenly queasy, her forehead hot… her mouth sourly beginning to water (and not in a good way) from the rusty metal tasting opening act of… of… she rolled down the window for air… and…

The chilled spring air, more slap than nudge… the wave of nausea averted… but disorientation remained.

After the posting, she'd be able to get some of the answers.

"You all right back there, ma'am… miss… Woods?

Agent Smith's voice was heard but it was the "Other Guy's" Rayban shielded eyes that stared at her in the rear view mirror. She nodded and rolled up the window with a shiver. The Other Guy turned on the heater and the blast of heat completed her re-entry into the present… and her laptop.

Meghan wrote that contrary to some reports, the FBI was more than all over this case and clearly was using their playbook of allowing local jurisdictions to squeeze the fruit for looking for seeds, while they stepped back for an aerial view to catch the eventual juice. And tho' Abby was convinced there was a legitimate threat, Meghan knew she was only part of the seeds, or at best pulp rather than any juice in a metaphor she was quickly losing control over…

No matter, she reasoned, Jan was right. The FBI and State Police of at least nine states were maybe only now beginning to know how big dot's ripple in their ponds was going to turn out to be. They still didn't have a name and Meghan could've guessed how many computer security consulting firms were being chased down to dead ends since last night. If, that part of dot's history turns out to be true, which, she reasoned, probably was…

"Fuck! " she exclaimed aloud, knowing that The Other Guy would be staring for the subject of that sentence, which she would ignore -- dot lessons were fucking working -- she would never be able to trust anything for what it seemed.

Especially here. They (the They will need to be explained when she edited before ever letting Jan see it) had played their hand when Officer Taylor showed up. They, (the Illinois State Authorities? More likely the Feds?) are as Jan had also told her, listening…

And it was hitting even harder that *they didn't have anything on dot but a confession.*

And the arraignment was coming,

and they would have to answer all of these questions before a judge.

And clearly… *they* were sweating.

The Detail, as Meghan had dubbed them, would be staying out of the Pen and they handed her off to the gruff but getting lovable escort after explaining to the morning gate clerk that no, these were not her boyfriends. The clerk and Meghan were the only ones who laughed at their joke, but then that's what they both expected and soon she was on her way…

And the question gnawed on her. What the fuck would she talk to dot about today?

Meghan was increasingly aware she had been playing for the enemy. Like the Native Scouts who led the white Cavalry through tribal lands, Meghan felt sick to her stomach to be "giving aid and comfort" even if it was indirectly. Her admiration for dot was right next to her revulsion. And oddly, today, she was okay with that.

Officer Taylor greeted her at the door, taking the handoff from 'Gruffy,' as Meghan had decided would be his name from now on, "Good Morning Ms. Woods."

Meghan clocked that Officer Taylor was freshly showered and ready for the day. She must have nighttime relief, Meghan reasoned, "Good Morning Officer Taylor, sleep well?" Officer Taylor nodded as she turned to take her position in the corner.

"She's lying. They don't even give the bitch a cot," Meghan turned to Officer Taylor for confirmation, who merely rolled her eyes. "Neither of us slept a wink, they keep the lights on when you say stupid things."

Meghan set up her recorder, "Unplanned consequences? You? Well knock me over with a feather."

When no snort, grunt, sigh, or snarky answer came, Meghan stood to peer into the cell. dot was sitting in the lotus position on the floor facing the wall opposite the wall with the entrance door that Meghan entered through every day. dot's face in profile revealed a rather large neck tattoo that Meghan hadn't noticed before and certainly hadn't expected: a snake whose tail draped over dot's left shoulder, and whose opened fanged mouth seemed poised to bite dot's left ear. dot must've sensed Meghan's stare, because she whispered, "Facing East."

Meghan jotted a note in her notebook and watched as dot's breathing slowed to a stone-like calm. Motionless, Meghan realized she was meditating. Officer Taylor crept closer to the window to check on her charge and shrugged to Meghan.

They all sat in silence for almost 10 minutes. dot was the first one to inhale deeply, then without opening her eyes, spoke gently, "Let's just say, consequences and leave it at that."

Meghan came out of a deep…. something. She had never meditated before, thought it was one of those things she should try someday, but this was… what? Exhaustion? Sleep deprivation? All of the above? Whatever brought her into the deepest calm she'd ever experienced, she wanted it again.

"Ten minutes of that will get you back on the right side of your day." dot was nowhere to be seen in the window's view, having shuffled off to her toilet. Officer Taylor was also trying to shake off whatever had just happened. She stood up with a start. And when she didn't see dot, hurried to the window in time to see dot walking back to her cot, "Welcome back Taylor, glad you could join us."

Officer Taylor instinctively looked up above the anti-cell door as if to see if she was in trouble. Meghan clocked it, but pretended to be checking her recorder when Officer Taylor turned to her. dot's voice boomed from the cot, "Taylor, we all know we're being watched, chill out… well, maybe not all the way out, this time."

Officer Taylor scowled at dot's window and walked back to her corner post without catching Meghan's eye. "C'mon Meghan, Illinois has two more days to make a case before a judge or the Feds are gonna yank me from them, so, you better make 'em count."

"Why East? You made a point of facing east to meditate."

dot smiled slightly, "Priorities. I like that. East is for enlightenment. West for wealth, North to ward off evil, South to control people. It's Vedic."

Meghan nodded and turned on her recorder, "How did you know James and Ronald would be together when the bibles were delivered? And how did you…"

"Whoa, girl, slow down, one at a time's all this little brain of mine can handle."

"Sorry."

"Those crazy boys can't keep their hands off each other. So I sent each a text from the other and let nature take its course."

"But there's so much that could've gone a different way!" Even Officer Taylor was startled by her frustration but sat forward for the answer nonetheless.

"Meghan. A soldier removes variables from the matrix of possible by steering toward probable."

"So, okay, horny little boys are somewhat predictable…"

"Even more so when they feel like they're in the protected class. Those boys sacrificed Kel to protect their own closet. And the problem was that they really enjoyed torturing another human."

"But, you're just playing into the right's narrative of sexual predators! They'll have a field day!"

"Look, closeted gay boys have always fucked this shit up – but except for that monster out in LA that was getting his dates meth'd up before murdering them, they've almost always been the Repubs. You're too young to remember the congressman who had a 'wide spread,' but we all know, and they do too, that the closet is a prison that always takes its toll. Why do you think they're trying so hard to force everyone back in? It's because it's the ultimate torture and they know from being there themselves and they want to use it. That's how sadistic these mutherfuckers are."

Meghan shook her head to clear the nasty buzzing of dot's words that had just violently shoved the sweet calm that had been there minutes before, "Ouch."

"Sorry, but it's true. They have known all along that we all are who we say we are, and that's what they use to punish us. They strip sunshine and acceptance from us. They *want* to skin us alive, cleave us from our identities, it's not that they want us to be like them. They want to have a biblically ordained get-out-of-jail-free card to be as fucking evil to another human as they can. They want us to be tormented in their hell."

Meghan couldn't help herself, "That's fucking dark as fuck."

"God Bless America. Did you get what you need? Or do you need more on that?"

Meghan checked her notes, "You burned down the church."

"Is that a question?"

"How is that going to send your message to the congregation?"

"Hmmm… you're right, too subtle?"

"But you said yesterday you wanted them to be looking over their shoulders and experiencing the fear that Kel experienced. This seems like the end of the story."

"If you say so."

"Well, what do you say?"

"I think I've said it."

Meghan waited for dot to pick up the thread. Silence. More silence. And more silence.

Meghan broke first, "But… I guess… well…"

"Awe honey, this is like making you eat broccoli. What do you think Christians do with all the hate they spew on a daily basis? It's basic physics. Their hatred is just acoustic waves, ripples of energy that flow out… until they hit something then, they rebound and flow back. In the quiet wee hours of the night, when they think their God himself, is asleep, they take their little dark fantasies and fears out and let them run around in their hearts… and when they do, they keep forgetting that those little pilot fishies latch onto the great white shark of doubt and all they'll see is their sanctuary burning, and they'll know they were never this enough or that enough or too much of this or that, to be worthy of their God's love, but they'll also know that truly… they are never safe. And if that doesn't work…"

Meghan sat-up, "Yes?"

"Well then, they're truly dead and no longer an issue. If you're not cut out for war, then you'll take the first chicken exit that comes. With no church to gather at, they'll have to decide to stay and rebuild or go somewhere else."

"But they'll be Martyrs."

"Not when they try to get a construction loan."

Meghan shook her head, "What do you know?"

"They have a number of lawsuits from other victims of their conversion therapy program. They'll never get a loan. Ever."

Meghan started to see how the mission was constructed. It was built on a cynical reality usually reserved for capitalists and politicians. A system used against itself according to its own rules. dot played a longer game than any one of her colleagues could have dreamed, certainly any of her enemies on the field of battle, "Did you put this much attention into your other victims?"

"Victims. We've had this discussion. Show me a little respect."

Meghan had never heard this tone before. Was dot slipping? "Begging your pardon, you prefer enemies? Did your enemies require this much attention, this many moving parts?

“As I said, each one is different. In some cases, their elimination was enough. In others, there were various ways to erase or at the very least minimize the damage they sought to cause.”

“For example?”

“The Nebraska Speaker of the House was a no-brainer. Once found, the FBI and NBI both shut down the Senate session. Many of them will term out before they get back to their stupidity, and the rest are fucking cowards who left the Freedom caucus once their families became pieces on the board.

“Pieces on the board?”

“Of course. You don’t think *they* thought for a minute it was going to end with the speaker, did you? They all knew they deserved what the speaker got and they are looking over their shoulders – but when 200 children all suddenly have security details like the one you got today, well, shit gets real, fast. And those who aren’t true believers will tuck their tails and head for that private sector that’s been promising them a payout for being good little boys and girls. Their families demand it. And the true believers, well they double down on their stupidity and soon the voters get wise.”

“Okay, since we’re on the subject of the Speaker, that seems like an odd duck in that he didn’t have direct blood on his hands like the Pastor did…”

“According to who?”

“Well, they don’t have a record…?”

“Meghan, honey… His bullshit notwithstanding, many children have been harmed in the name of that piece of… legislature, so, the blood, hands, thingy, will as you say be directly traced to him. The continued toxicity of the environment where these incredible idiots believe they have license to let hate fly has also been solidified by his treachery, but more importantly, he stared into the eyes of trans children and their parents and not only ignored their pleas for common decency, he lied to the one legislator who had held out against their political games and said, your child’s life, *because they’re trans,* does not matter here.”

“I… uh, okay, “ stammered Meghan, “I agree that he and others like him are responsible, but they have a degree of separation, at least according to precedent…”

dot waited patiently for Meghan’s words to stop bouncing around the anti-cell then stated flatly, “Yeah, these clowns actually believe that they can write laws around morality, we all know that sending our young to war is pulling the trigger directly. And, I’m not trying them in a court of law.”

“So, you see yourself as judge and jury.”

“Problem with that? You have been shackled by their indoctrination. I have not. I am no judge. I am no jury. I am removing assets from the battlefield.”

“As you’ve said… forgive me, but I have not been able to obtain the official charges against you…”

“Because there are as of yet, none.”

"Yes, so, for the article, how many murders, er enemies have you removed from the battlefield? How many did you confess to killing when you turned yourself in?"

"47? Yes."

"Was that all of them?"

"No. But it was enough to convince them."

"You said the Feds will step in if the Illinois Attorney General…"

"When. When the Illinois Attorney General…"

"Thank you *when* the Illinois Attorney can't make a case. You turned yourself in. Why not help them with your name and anything else they need?"

"If they want a conviction, they have to do the work, otherwise the Grand Jury will just set me free."

"Sounds like you want to be convicted."

"As I said. I can't accomplish my mission the way I was going about it. I'm playing whack-a-mole with the lunacy and stupidity of humanity. How long can you keep advocating for your own humanity, Meghan? How long must we all fight for just decent human respect?"

"They're going to argue that by your own actions, you have given up that right."

"You can't give up what you don't have."

Meghan conceded dot's point with a nod. She turned her pages and scanned her notes, "There's speculation that you are Queer, but few reporters have made the jump to Trans. Was that your plan? Doesn't everyone need to know that these crimes against Trans people are being avenged by a Trans woman?"

"It was leaked that I was Trans and both the FBI and the State Police in all of the jurisdictions are not subtle. Their questioning is trying to find info on a Trans woman. It's out there. And it's not avenging…"

"But doesn't this ambiguity make it hard on any would-be supporters or allies?"

"I don't need allies…"

"BUT WE DO! WHAT ABOUT US? WE'RE GOING TO BE…

… LEFT… to deal… with their wrath… yet again, while… while you're rotting in some prison."

Even Officer Taylor was shocked by Meghan's outburst. dot walked forward to the window and stared compassionately at Meghan, "Honey. Do you have everything you need?"

Meghan shut off her recorder, "I… might not need to come tomorrow. I'm going to get this ready for posting in the morning. If I need anything else, I'll come back in the afternoon."

dot nodded, "Of course. Take care of yourself."

Officer Taylor stood and walked Meghan to the door. They exchanged a wordless glance and Meghan waited as the door announced with its iron and steel throat that she was leaving.

The FBI Agents were waiting beside the clerk's window as Meghan came to retrieve her cell phone, "She called it early, did she? Hope you got what you needed?" Meghan caught the clerk's slip, "I still have one more day, right?" The clerk nodded, "You have as long as the Warden said you had. That's between you and her. Above my pay grade, you know."

Meghan slid behind her pokerface and turned to Agent Smith, "Have you guys been waiting here all this time for me?" She knew the answer, she just wanted to see how they spun it. Agent Smith smiled professionally which was creepy, making Meghan wish he had stayed in stoic mode, "We were… here to…"

"Save it, Agent Smith. Let's just keep it professional, shall we?" She nodded to the desk clerk and waited for Gruffy to open the gate. The Agents followed her to the Escalade. Now, in the cold light of day, she saw that there was an even thinner line between the FBI and Gangsta Rappers, the only thing missing were spinners and sick beats.

Meghan waited patiently for the other Agent to open her door, who she clocked, still hadn't introduced himself. Once in, she put in her air pods and opened her notebook. Her plan had made sense until her exit. She knew she was in good shape on her article and today's interview was supposed to be short; all she needed was to get dot on the record for the number of killings, knowing her tally and the FBI's was going to greatly differ.

But now Meghan wasn't sure if she was just being petulant, but she hate, hate, hated to be pushed around or manipulated. She had played by the rules until she graduated from High School. Honor roll, student-athlete, admitted to college. Meghan kept her nose clean, lived up to everyone's expectations, and made her parents proud.

Then Meghan came out.

And learned how everyone actually felt about her. About her community. About being Trans. It took a while, but eventually, Meghan was grateful they had made it so easy. She had to cut them off and out of her life. They could have their rules, but they couldn't have her life.

Just like they were trying to do to her now.

She was being used. Whoever was listening in on their conversations treated them both as weird strange confusing creatures that required Meghan's skills to translate dot's words. It was infuriating. And astounding. The mental gymnastics required to keep her and dot and all of her siblings as dot would say, required nurturing. Constant attention like tending a poisonous plant. It would start to wither when her humanity shined on it. So they would water it with their own venom and manufactured confusion. She had seen her own father beat down his love for her by reminding himself that straight, and therefore normal people had all agreed that they weren't *supposed* to understand her, 'and her kind' until he himself became the victim, who had lost his son, chip off the ol' block, his god-given legacy.

And it made her sick in the pit of her stomach.

Ironically, Meghan knew the interior processes that her father had gone through intimately. The same denial that she used to get through the first 25 years of her life in the wrong body, was the one her father used on himself every day since she told him she was his daughter. Pretending. Pretending everything's okay. Pretending you're right. Pretending it will all go away. And when it doesn't… eventually, it collapses.

She had had a special relationship with her father before she came out. Meghan and her father could look each in the eye and check the other on their bullshit. "Never bullshit a bullshitter" she had been taught. So it was maddening that he was going against everything he himself had taught her. He was bullshitting himself. And cutting her out of his heart.

Meghan saw that she was being studied by Agent Smith in the rearview mirror. She pulled out her earpod to hear, "I'm sorry?"

Agent Smith shrugged, "I didn't say anything." Meghan shrugged back, and replaced her airpod, keeping her eyes on the mirror. Agent Smith looked back to the road.

Meghan had drawn the line at allowing them to come into her apartment, knowing now that she was the threat, she would not help them with their sham. It took Abby an hour of negotiating to get them to stand down, which Lucas speculated was enough time to set up a trace of their lines and computers.

Meghan wanted to say that Lucas was being paranoid, but couldn't be 100 percent sure they weren't right. She was up til after midnight typing, snacking on the sweet potato chips that Lucas made in their air fryer, and sipping the last of the sparkling apple juice in the fridge. She had a workable draft to bring to Jan in the morning. Jan would make sure Meghan had nailed it before her time with dot ran out.

On nights like this, Meghan only slept an hour at a time, waking up almost to the minute, reminding herself that sleep was the best use of her time, and then just grazing REM sleep state before snapping awake yet again. At six am she finally decided she'd had enough, and showered, dressed, kissed Lucas goodbye and headed out. Agent Smith and "the Other Guy" which is what Meghan decided would be his name in her article, were waiting as if they'd been monitoring her. She put on a cheery smile and wished them good morning as she skipped down the steps.

The Other Guy opened the door for Meghan, standing aside as she buckled herself in. She texted Jan that she was inbound and read over her article on her laptop one more time.

8

"

... too heinous to be tried by only one state.

"

"It's good. It's thorough and... she's... interesting."

"But...?" queried Meghan as Jan, red pen in hand slashed and struck what Meghan couldn't see.

"But?" said Jan as she set the pile of paper on her immaculate desk, "But nothing. You know it's good, I'm confirming. Don't read into it."

Meghan relaxed, "If it needs anything, today's our last chance."

Jan turned to Agent Smith and "The Other Guy," chuckling as she thought about Meghan's name for him, "I'm pretty sure, we're good, but lemme take it to legal, directly. Get some coffee, I'll sit with them as they read it through. You wanna have some fun, take your detail to Starby's."

Meghan smiled at the thought, but she was already an outsider here at the office. Still, a decent dose of caffeine would be the ticket, "You want some?" Jan waved her Vente Iced Coffee as an answer and winked, grabbed the papers, and headed for legal.

Jan was right, it was fun. Agent Smith and The Other Guy ordered Chai Lattes and Meghan was listening for The Other Guy's real name to be announced by the barista, but Agent Smith had done the ordering, so he was going to be The Other Guy, for now. Meghan's tall drip with four added shots was finally ready and they were on their way back when her phone's news notifications started flooding in. She was reading as they entered the elevator when the Agents' phones started blowing up as well.

"You gonna check that?" grinned Meghan, knowing at least why their phones wouldn't shut up, but neither would dare a peek with her this close. Agent Smith stared ahead, back in stoic mode, "No ma'am."

They were back on the thirtieth floor when Meghan released them back to their post outside Jan's office. She entered the office and started to read her bulletins. The state of Illinois had lost its fight to keep dot before they even got to argue their case. dot's crimes, it seemed were too heinous to be tried by only one state. Her public defender hadn't even successfully presented a petition for any defense of her rights and there was no way the Feds were going to let her walk from one case for fear it would set precedent.

Jan came into her office, face flushed. "Well, thank god you've got the drop on everyone. We're still a complete feature, whereas theirs are all mere 'spectaculationing.' Where's their self-respect?"

Meghan stood, "You said it yourself, they're obviously leaking our conversations."

"Yes, but even an idiot could see that nobody, from the Feds on down hasn't the slightest clue who they're dealing with. And reposting their leaks just shines a spotlight on their bumbling."

Meghan tried to sip her coffee, but discovered she'd drained it without even knowing it, "I guess, a story's always only as good as it's OTR source."

Jan started to laugh, "Well, if these dumbasses aren't using AI to write their crap, then maybe they should start. Legal is saying we've got a green light to go exclusive. Once your full story is out there, others are going to pile on and/or steal from us instead, but at least it'll be accurate… in light of this change of venue, we think you'll be able to do follow-up without needing her direct quotes.

Meghan her empty cup into Jan's overflowing wastebasket, "That's good, since they'll obviously cut off everyone's access to her."

"Barndoor after the pony bolts," Jan picked up the wastebasket and showed it into the hall outside her office, then closed her door, "you'll have broken the story, it's academic after that. Think you got enough for now to fill until she gets her federal trial?"

It was happening fast, "Of course," lied Meghan, not exactly sure what she was even lying about, "There's going to be at least 47 charges of murder plus the ancillary tag-ons that AG's looking to make their careers love. When will it post?"

"We've got the entire editorial staff proofing it. Minutes?"

Meghan sat down on the couch where Jan had spent more of her career than her own apartment, catching an hour between deadlines. "So… what do I do now?"

"Don't you usually meet up with Lucas and drink too many Margaritas to celebrate your postings?"

"Yes, but it's not even lunchtime." Both Agents jumped to standing, phones to their ears as if they were connected. They stared off as if getting a briefing. They were tense, battle ready. Meghan walked out into the hallway with Jan on her tail.

Both Agents looked confused. They looked to Meghan and then back into space, "Uh, but chief… who is… well Sir, she's been under our… yes sir. Thank you, sir."

Agent Smith put his phone away, "Um, well, Ms. Woods, it's thought that the Inmate's being moved to Federal Custody lessens the threat to you."

"Bullshit," said Jan laughing, the rest of the staff piled out of their offices to see why she was using expletives with FBI Agents, "Guys. Seriously? You can be happy that you get to give up your babysitting job and get back to real Special Agenting action. You have an organic excuse to end your dinner theater. "

The Agents put on their sunglasses as they nodded goodbye and left. Jan turned to the rest of the staff, then to Meghan, "It's only one story people, we've got a few hundred gigs between ads to fill," Jan shrugged to Meghan with a laughed, "It's only one story, but it's one hell of a story."

Meghan stood on the street. Lucas was going to be tied-up until five with meetings at the Children's Hospital, they promised to get away as soon as they could. Hanging around at the office was the absolute worst way to wait for the posting, and she was no longer hungry.

Meghan found herself walking to the EL.

What was she doing? She was numb, raw, really, she knew she was getting better as a writer, but seriously? Jan didn't have one single note. It was surreal. Even legal let it through on what her father would call 'greased skids.'

She sat on the westbound train, opened her laptop, and there it was, "Geezus, true crime beats the hell outta local Politics." She started reading. She had some incendiary stuff in there, stuff that rightwing trolls die for, which always made her cringe when she read someone else's account. What was she supposed to do?

Yes, she was the only 'credible rep' in the newsroom that

should've written it. Meghan's byline gave Asphere the blue check of 'plausible reasonableness' to balance dot's extreme 'dotness'. No one will be able to question her or Asphere's bias, while also passing the street cred test.

'Lived-experience bonofides' had become coin of the realm in a news environment continually being swallowed by billionaires with conservative agendas, especially in matters concerning the Queer community, lest they become political talking points. Ever since the great polarization of 2023, as Meghan had written, when right-led boycotts exposed corporate cowardice and befuddlement in dealing with LGBTQIA2S+ issues, like Anheuser Busch & Target's instant capitulation to their "canceling" by right-wing buyers, most "credible" News sources were either exposed for their right-wind editorial slant, believing that they were no longer constrained by "the social contract." Or guessing that the tides had shifted and preemptively veered right. And guessing wrong. And losing subscribers. But doubling down. And losing more subscribers. And reporters. And ratings. And advertising dollars.

But Asphere had figured out long before the other news sites, *audiences* were not the same as subscribers. Subscribers demanded the accuracy Right, Central or Left. Subscribers paid the bills. Audiences did not. And Meghan was the accurate choice for the byline.

Which, Meghan believed was not a bad thing. Sure, she hoped one day to write about other things that made her human, but for now, it was as all-consuming for her as it apparently was for the right-wing third of the country.

But also while she wasn't going to sell out her community, *ever*, she also wasn't going to stand back and let it be hijacked by murder and violence either. She was sensitive to the trend of false equivalencies even by the left by insecure writers begging for legitimacy. dot had been very good at appearing rational and maybe even right in looking at this as a war and applying the rules of engagement, but… No, Meghan thought, murder is still murder.

And that was how dot was going to be viewed in a court of law, even though that same court had been systemically looking through the cisgender lens at Transgender issues…

Which… made Megan pause. dot was right, they were at war. The firestorm of State and Federal bills, numbering in the hundreds, taking up almost half of all bills written in the last year just to hack the system against the Trans community, like redefining life as only having two sexes, (not genders) defined by chromosomes and "sex assigned at birth" (ignoring that it was scientifically inaccurate) the delegitimizing lived experience by labeling it "gender idealogy" and describing Trans women as "biological males" was a confessed and celebrated effort toward complete erasure. And it was unrelenting.

And… working. At least it could appear to be,

And with it came the micro aggressions and real world discrimination that threatened a future of *never* for Trans people. Never equal. Never at peace. Never perceived as human.

Meghan stopped her rabbitholing before it swallowed her.

But murder? *Murder*-murder?

dot had been terrifyingly vicious in her attacks, designed to degrade her victims as much as they had degraded their victims. Her mind kept trying to rationalize it into the usual aphorisms like violence begets violence, and hell hath no fury… the type of phrases that usually are said with a sigh of surrender in the voice; a weak exasperation of an uncontested inevitability that never advanced toward change.

Because wasn't that the point? Of dot's mission? Of her own writing? Of… life?

But… as much as she told herself she was the one to write it, it kept gnawing at her… there was really only one reason she was ultimately there…

… dot had *wanted* her there.

A cold wash of dread crawled from Meghan's head to her toes. Why? Really, why? She kept rereading her article, searching for the answer, or at least a clue… some bread crumb…

Meghan kept scrutinizing her article -- and was still convinced she hadn't helped to make dot a folk heroine. She had painted a fair and accurate portrait of the person who had stared at her from the window, even describing the tattoo in such a way as to not inspire others or glorify dot, but as a way to demonstrate the intensity and extremes this woman was willing to go.

Meghan was also sure she hadn't made dot's Transness the issue, nor the reason for her crimes other than her, "best defense is a helluva good offense" defense, which *should* be dot's actual legal defense if and when she would get one. Not that anything she wrote or her eventual attorneys would defend, would actually keep conservatives from regarding dot or her community as anything other than mentally ill, but she never wanted to give them any fuel for that fire.

But it was hard to defend the point of dot's war.

Meghan read aloud the block quote that Jan had selected for the intro, *"It was why, she left no doubt to the severity and morality of her intent. Each victim had a clear and obvious price paid for the violence they had committed against dot's siblings and extended rainbow family. It was personal to her."*

As her voice slapped back off the EL's scratched and dingy window her breath caught in her throat, "Fuck." It was all there, the Asphere editorial team hadn't changed a word. She continued to scroll, reading…

dot adamantly refused to even consider backing down or away from the hard line she seared into the sand. She freely conceded that no one would, could or even should regard her actions as anything other than extremely cold, calculating and abhorrent. She made no apology, freely accepting consequences and the wall she had built between her and forgiveness.

Meghan chewed on the words, loving that she was getting drawn into her own writing, as the memories of the Pastor's death suddenly slashed Meghan's awareness, the horror of his last moments as he died symbolically crushed by the fiery weight of the bible that set his skin ablaze. The other crime scenes of which she had only seen the photos, seemed like short horror films, they moved in her memories, the victims, the Speaker of the Nebraska House, the owners & bouncers of the Las Perlas restaurant, the Texas rednecks who died the way they killed having been dragged behind their own truck, and others living out their last moments in lurid detail in Meghan's consciousness.

Some of the other deaths which dot had confessed, were known to Meghan and the culties, like the three men in Texas who were made to run several miles as they had once made a lonely teenage Trans girl run one humid July night. But when the truck they were tied to speeded up right as they were passing the police station, fatigue finally claimed their footing and they fell. The truck circled three times passing shoppers and diners on Main Street before the police knew what was happening… by the time they caught up, the truck had been abandoned next to the fence where the teen had originally been found and all that was left of the three strapping twenty-year-old "good Christian boys, who had bright futures cut off" could be put into one body bag.

"Jeezus, was this price of freedom?" Meghan's question was swallowed by the squeal of the EL's brakes as it came to the end of the line station. She stood and walked off the train and automatically down the stairs, to catch a rideshare to the Pen, "That time when I had a protection detail," she laughed was only just this morning.

9

"

Something tells me this book has never been its cover.

"

The clerk wasn't surprised to see her back, despite her pseudo-goodbye yesterday. Gruffy escorted her upstairs like he always had.

As they ascended the last of the stairs, Meghan was still not sure why she was there. She was sleepwalking in a nightmare of which there seemed no end. The door's opening startled even Gruffy. Two Federal Marshalls escorted dot as she shuffled between them, shackled at the waist and ankles. Gruffy pulled Meghan physically to the cell side of the catwalk, "We let 'em pass," he croaked, Meghan clocked that this was the first time she heard his voice. dot, eyes down, passed slowly glancing at

Meghan. They locked eyes. Without the scratched and grimy glass between them, Meghan realized she had been wrong about her eyes, they were blue.

dot was escorted down the stairs and into a door that Meghan had never been through, but then, they never gave her a tour when she had arrived. Meghan slumped against the railing, was this a wasted trip or was she being given her own sense of closure? She sighed, shrugged with surrender, and looked to Gruffy who nodded and escorted her back down the stairs to her own processing out.

Meghan held the cold steel railing, her feet knew where to walk they just didn't know why. She didn't know why she had come and now she didn't know why she was leaving… she only knew something was… really wrong.

The desk clerk handed Meghan back her iPhone, and Meghan could see dot on the bank of surveillance monitors on the wall behind. A Marshall's hand on her head, dot was backed into the back of the beige Dodge Challenger with a Marshall's star on the door. "There goes your girl," narrated the desk clerk as she pushed the sign-in sheet under the bulletproof glass partition for Meghan's initials.

Meghan saw the Challenger start to pull away in one monitor then scanned the other monitors as she tried to track it's journey. One last time? For "old time's sake?" The foggy dread was starting to lift, leaving only a nagging thread, like an errant hair from your bangs that keeps getting caught in your mascara; annoying but not so much that you actually fix it you just keep blowing it out of your way.

She was mesmerized by the monitors, vaguely aware that yes, they had been there the whole time, but somehow, maybe the pressure being off, she reasoned, she could take in everything else? And it wasn't just dot's departure but all of the views of the Pen. Maybe she was aware this might be what Jan foretold, her last time in a place that most likely would be a defining moment in her career. "Boy, you don't even wait for the body to cool before you fill-up the cell again, do ya?"

The desk clerk turned and stared at the monitors. Sure enough, a person was lying on the cot in dot's cell. The desk clerk radioed up to the top floor guard to have a look. Meghan and the desk clerk watched as a guard walked down the catwalk and buzzed open dot's cell then entered the anti-cell. They watched as the guard walked up to dot's cell and look inside the window. She opened the cell door and Officer Taylor stood up. Her eyes blackened and bruised, The guard's voice crackled over the radio, "Officer down, officer down!"

For Meghan it was like an action movie playing out across the twenty or so screens, each showing the story unfold. Alarms started wailing. On one screen several officers could be seen scrambling into cars in the garage and racing out after the Marshall. They could be heard trying to reach the Marshall's car via radio. On another screen, a helicopter was spinning up its blades as four armed guards piled in. But nothing was adding up. Why would dot do this, and how could the Marshalls not notice an officer was hurt...?

On one screen in the lower left, Meghan watched as Officer Taylor lying on a gurney was wheeled down a hallway into a room marked Infirmary.

On the top screen, the helicopter lifted off and Meghan could feel the rumble of its power rock the Pen's walls. She imagined a highspeed chase would soon be written about on the web, but why the need for the helicopter if dot was in the custody of the Marshalls?

"Ambulance needed for the infirmary." The lower left screen showed a gurney being wheeled out of the infirmary. She could see Officer Taylor wasn't doing well, her purple eyes swelling over the rim of an oxygen mask, two attendants rushing her down the corridor to the…

… garage. And into a waiting ambulance. The Ambulance sped out of the garage.

The desk clerk raised an eyebrow to Meghan, "It's a fucking circus here today." Meghan shook her head. "Well, I guess that means I have the rest of the day off?" The desk clerk roared with laughter. It broke the spell and Meghan realized whatever was going on, being inside the Pen today might not be such a great idea.

"Safe and sound," declared the driver as she pulled up to the EL station. Meghan thanked the driver and was getting out of her car when her phone rang. It was Lucas, "Babe are you okay?"

"Yes,… sorry, I just got back to the EL, I wanted… I dunno, to say goodbye to dot… or something."

"She's dead. At least they think she's dead."

"What the fuck?" Meghan put Lucas on speaker as she scrolled through her feed, a news helicopter showed the wreckage of a Marshall's car and two Pen guard cars, still burning, three body bags… first responders milling about. "Babe… I'm going to need a ride home… come and get me in two hours?"

Meghan turned in time to hail the rideshare she had just gotten out of. The driver pulled around and she hopped back in. She showed her the video footage from her phone, "Do you know where this is? It's on the road leading away from the Pen." The driver, a woman in her fifties looked closer at the phone, "Yeah? It's…" The helicopter went in a complete circle, trees, and riverappearing in the background, "Maybe the Des Plains… yeah. Des Plains River."

There was so much air traffic that it wasn't that hard to find. The driver offered to stay, obviously caught up in the drama and Meghan was grateful. She hiked out into the crime scene taking notes in her notebook. An FBI Agent clocked her and within seconds she had a tap on her shoulder, "Ms. Woods."

She turned to see The Other Guy, FBI Field vest on, aviator shades covering his eyes, "Agent…"

"Lincoln, ma'am."

"So you do have a voice."

"Not much to say, ma'am. Can I help you?"

"As a matter of fact, yes. Is there an incident commander or media liaison, I just need a statement."

Agent Lincoln stared around. Meghan wasn't sure if he was looking for help for her or for him, she also wasn't sure that she liked that suddenly The Other Guy had a name. Whatevs, he waved her to follow him. They walked through the wreckage to where Agent Smith and three other FBI Agents were talking. A coroner was stooping over the bodies and snapping photos of each's injuries, then zipping up the bags. Meghan felt queasy that he was able to get all up in their grills, then zip up the bag without a second thought.

"Benny, got a fangirl here."

Agent Smith turned to see Meghan and his shoulder slumped. He took another deep breath of professionalism, filled up his chest, and stepped forward, "Ms. Woods. How can I help?" Meghan smiled, trying to keep from fainting as the coroner struggled with the last zipper, "Agent Smith… I'm… excuse me…" The coroner finally succeeded and dot's bloodied head and shoulders spilled out.

Meghan swooned and Agent Smith caught her. He helped her away from the bodies as the other Agents tried to maintain decorum, "You need a hand there Benjamin?" Meghan caught herself and stood weakly out of the Agent's support, "I'm fine. Thank… you." The coroner turned dot's face from side to side snapping pics of the damage. "She must've hit her head, her features distorted, crushed bone and shredded flesh," declared the coroner into a handheld recorder. "Victim suffered impact trauma, there is broken glass embedded in the impact wound along with soil and asphalt abrasions, speculation: victim was thrown through the windshield."

Agent Smith stood close to make sure Meghan was steady, "You good?" Meghan nodded and sighed. She watched as the coroner zipped dot back into the body bag, "She hit so hard she lost her tattoo."

"What did you say?"

Meghan shook her head, and vomited at Agent Smith's feet. He jumped in time. "Reflexes like a Cat!" "Bojangles!" and "Get ya some!" were almost drowned out by Agent Smith's, "Oh! No, you don't!"

Meghan wiped her mouth with her sleeve. "Sorry." Agent Smith had escaped, shoes unscathed, "what did you say? Something about a tattoo?"

Meghan shook off the queasiness, "dot has a huge snake tattoo on her neck and left shoulder that looks like it's biting her left ear."

Agent Smith turned to the coroner who was packing away his camera, "Hey Seikosan, the vic there have any identifying tattoos?" The coroner stopped and looked at the three body bags, "Which one?"

Meghan interrupted, "The last one, that one there." She pointed to the smaller of the three. The coroner shook his head, "No. Nothing visible. I'll be doing a full 'topsey' when I get 'em back to my lab." Agent Smith turned to Meghan, "He says no."

Meghan had gotten back her bearings, "Then you got the wrong dot." Agent Smith stared at her blankly. Meghan nodded, "You got the wrong dot. Holy shit. dot you fucking bitch ass, Queen."

Agent Smith snapped on some latex gloves and unzipped the smaller body bag. He studied both sides of the corpse's freshly shaved head. It was hideous, a pornographic mass of violated flesh, blood, and dirt. But no tattoo. It had never had a tattoo.

He zipped it back up and checked the other two body bags, the Marshalls had each had their faces torn off when the body bags deployed. One had had what used to be the lower jaw dangling by a thin strand of cartilage, the other the nose shoved into the brain, mercifully killing him instantly… but no tattoos."

He snapped off the latex gloves with impatience and disdain, pulling out his cell phone, "Chief… I need a mug shot of ISI W10042574. Yeah, I got a credible witness who… well, let me check then I'll fill you in if it's anything."

The text notification came in almost instantly, Agent Lincoln looked over his shoulder as they studied the pic, "What's with the fuzziness, come on Illy." The left side profile showed dot's snake in all its glory, mouth mockingly wide like it was laughing. Agent Smith dropped his arms to his side in defeat, "Fucking Hell." He turned to Meghan, "Alright, let's lock it down. Lock it all down. No one in or out. Get it all, boys." The Agents all donned gloves and what had been a routine traffic accident only minutes before, was now an active crime scene.

Meghan would learn from Agent Lincoln that the Marshall's car near as they could tell had tried to outrun the Prison Guards, which was odd in itself, but when the guards executed a pincher move, aided by the huge rotor wash from the helicopter, the Marshalls' car had flipped onto its side, before ramming one of the Guard's cars in the rear igniting the gas tank.

The guards had all survived with injuries but the cars were destroyed. Nobody had an answer yet why the chase had started. Agent Smith chimed in that it's standard Marshall's procedure that once they depart with a transport everyone is an enemy of the state. An unfortunate clash of training and jurisdictions.

Meghan called Jan while she waiting to be allowed to leave. The breaking news of the crash was the best way to launch the full article and already Meghan's star was rising. That she was on the scene for the breaking news was a gift. Meghan whispered the news of the tattoo to Jan, taking three times for her to understand what she was saying.

"Meghan? Are you fuc… that's unfuc… How the fuc…!?!?!?" Jan excitedly promised to write up the update, with Meghan's byline of course.

As Meghan was reading the draft for accuracy, dots passing her on the catwalk flashed into her head. Her eyes, blue… blue… no! That's when she realized, she should've seen the tattoo then, It wasn't even dot when they escorted her out…

"Jan. Record my voice."

"But can't you do it?"

"There's an embargo here – hurry! At the Pen, an Officer Taylor had been assigned as suicide watch…."

"Yes, I read your article."

"Jan. Please. When I got to the Pen today, two Marshalls were escorting dot from her cell. As she passed, we locked eyes, which was the first time we got to look at each other without the window in our way. I always thought her eyes were hazel but today they were cobalt blue, which distracted me from seeing that dot didn't have a tattoo. When I got downstairs to the security monitoring area, I could see in dot's cell that someone was locked in, just minutes after dot had been moved, it turned out to be Officer Taylor! She was bruised severely, and was taken by ambulance…"

"So you think that was in fact, dot."

"I don't know what to think anymore, but something tells me this book has never been its cover."

"Honey, it's a weird metaphor, we can work on that later, I'll start digging."

Agent Lincoln could see that Meghan was not where he left her and hiked into the trees. Meghan got her cell turned off in time to sit and make it look like she had a rock in her shoe.

"Ms. Woods. We'd appreciate it if you stay up near your ride home."

"And Agent Lincoln, I appreciate it if you'd let me avail myself of said ride home. I believe I have helped immensely today, and I'm rather tired.

"It won't be long ma'am."

10

"

I was going to say spooky, but you'd redline the hell out of that…

"

He lied. It was another two hours before the FBI was willing to release everyone. The rideshare driver was only too happy to drive Meghan the hour and fifteen minutes to her home, knowing that Asphere was picking up the tab. But truly speaking, the driver was fond of Meghan and would've driven her home for free, exhilarated to be part of something so out-of-the-ordinary.

Meghan was minutes from her home when her phone rang, "Ms. Woods, Agent Smith. I'm curious… may I ask *why* you were out at the Pen today?"

Meghan still wasn't sure why she went, but she for sure knew now why she was there, and was about to say as much, when she answered, “I wanted dot to hear from me first that the article was going to post.”

“And why was that important Ms. Woods?”

“Well, Agent Smith, I suppose if you were in the journalism business, you’d understand. File it under professional courtesy and best practices, if you need a reason.”

“Goodnight Ms. Woods.”

“Goodnight, Agent Smith.”

She thanked the driver and exchanged numbers for any future follow-up and Meghan trekked up the stairs with the last fumes of energy she had and fell into Lucas’ arms.

Lucas was up early making a hearty breakfast. They had practically carried Meghan to a drawn hot bath, poured a half glass of celebratory champagne down her throat then carried her to bed. She had slept in her big terry cloth robe, hair still wrapped in the towel.

The smell of coffee and vegan bacon was alluring, but Meghan couldn’t will her eyelids open. She had been completely drained. Then the day’s images started flooding her brain as if someone had been standing on the hose, then suddenly stepped off. Shattered fragments competed for her attention like kindergarteners who had been asked about their favorite pet; A snake tattoo, dot’s blue piercing eyes, Officer Taylor’s bruised and swollen eyes, no snake tattoo. Body bags. Burning bibles.

Agent Smith. Agent Lincoln. A snake tattoo again.

Meghan reached for her phone and opened the app for the Asphere Publishing site. Jan had been busy, and the front page follow-up to Meghan's profile of dot credited her with the news from yesterday. She scanned the article and saw that it was almost verbatim to her message to Jan, except for a follow-up of the local hospitals… Officer Taylor hadn't been checked in anywhere. Further, her employee profile at the Pen listed her as a newly hired contract employee with one of 20 agencies that provided support services to the state Penal system.

Meghan laughed out loud, "Of course she is." Lucas entered with a tray, "Breakfast in bed for the Woman of the hour." Meghan rub the sleep from her eyes to see hot coffee, pancakes, bacon, and even a bird of paradise, "Nipped fresh from the Anderson's hedge." Meghan set her phone down so Lucas could spoil her properly, kissing their nose as they leaned in to set the tray over her lap.

As she happily munched bacon and slurped her expertly made latte, "Puttin' those barista skills to work, bro," Meghan brought them up to speed. "No one is willing to go on record yet, but dot… and Officer Taylor has effectively… vanished."

Lucas stole a bite of bacon from Meghan's hand, "So… they no longer have a suspect in custody for the crimes that had been linked together by dot's confessions. Watching the fallout and spin from this one is going to be better than the finale of Game of Thrones."

Meghan fed Lucas the last bite of her pancake, handed them the tray, and stood up. Lucas could see her mind was already spinning, and their thoughtful breakfast was working its magic. She downed the last of her latte and headed for the shower, doubled back, and kissed Lucas passionately, “You are the best thing that’s ever happened to me ever.” She spun and headed to the shower for real this time.

The entire staff of Asphere was gathered in the conference room watching the news feed on the widescreen when Meghan stepped out of the elevator. She didn’t even take off her coat or backpack as she wove her way in beside Jan who kept her eyes on the screen while hugging her hello. An aerial shot of the Pen revealed that the protestors had remained and had grown since the news, broken by Meghan’s article revealed that dot was Trans. A banner across the top of the frame declared, “Breaking News. IDC Press Conference.”

They all murmured amongst themselves as the view switched to a spokesperson, a middle-aged white man with a crewcut and almost pink skin covered by an embroidered polo shirt from the Illinois Department of Corrections. He stepped up to a podium, flanked by uniformed officers of several agencies, “Thank you. Good Morning. Yesterday, a person being transferred by the Federal Marshall’s office from the Stateville Correctional Facility escaped custody…”

The room where the Press conference was being held erupted in flashes and murmurs, the Spokesperson waited for the flurry to subside. “During the incident, three people were killed and two are missing. We are working in a joint task force with the FBI and IBI to resolve this as quickly as possible and without further injury. This person is presumed armed and extremely dangerous, we are circulating photos of the suspect, drawing your attention to the identifying tattoo on the left neck and asking that anyone with any information to please call the tip line that will be… is it? Yes? Yes, appearing on your screen and the incident command website. That is all I have to say at this time. Thank you."

A flurry of questions was shouted at the Spokesperson, but the entire phalanx of police and corrections officers and agents followed him back into the Pen.

Meghan's phone rang as Jan turned to her to confer. Meghan saw the caller ID: Agent Smith FBI, and showed it to Jan who grabbed her and led her toward her office for privacy. Meghan answered on speaker phone as Jan closed the door, "This is Meghan Woods, good morning Agent Smith….

"Good morning, Meghan. Having fun yet?"

The voice was not Agent Smith's, "Um…" and then a chill ripped through Meghan's body, "dot?" She looked at the caller ID again, and shook her head to Jan, setting her phone down gingerly as if it were a bomb.

"I suppose I have you to thank since that's going to be my name going forward. I was thinking of pronouncing it *period*, you know, like end of sentence or thought. But since your article, the die is cast. Everyone's following your lead, congratulations as the kids would say, you're trending."

"Did you… is Agent Smith all right?"

"I guess that's a fair assumption, either that or I stole his phone, which, given his annoyance with all things that tether him to another human, would have not been hard, and I guess unless you know about spoofing. Which, I leave to you as to whether you take the time to relate that to your readers."

Meghan looked to Jan, "Well, yes, there's a shit ton of questions that…"

"Honey. You know as well as I do that if anyone knew you and I were talking, your life would be… very complicated. Your credibility only remains if you stay neutral and describe first-hand accounts, or like your friend Jan, there, Hi Jan, did by following up on your first-hand accounts."

Jan and Meghan looked around the room for cameras they both looked like mice caught without cover knowing the owl was only a talon away. "The phone. It's the phone, ladies. Just because you don't see the camera's on, doesn't mean it's not."

They both shook their heads. "So here's the deal, they're going to chase their tail, unsuccessfully for several weeks. They will get frustrated, several people will be fired and then they will be ripe for interviewing. Ego and fear will tenderize them to start selling each other out. You'll know who the players are and it will be very easy for you to follow your leads. I don't expect you to make your career out of me, because who wants to be that girl? But I'll be watching and if you need to talk to me, I'll make myself… available."

"But what about Officer Taylor? And who was that in your body bag?"

"Weren't you the one who said this book was never its cover?"

Meghan sat down hard. "How the fuck…?"

dot sighed audibly. "Jan, do you want to tell her or should I?"

Jan thought about it a moment and then it dawned, "I put your quote into the article."

"Public knowledge, and all."

"So, but, same for Officer Taylor."

"Is that a statement or a question?"

"Question?"

"Like I said, you'll need to be able to back up your own assertions with eyewitness accounts or research. Until next time, dear. Jan, you got a gem there, treat her well."

The call ended and they both took their first breaths in several minutes, but it was short-lived. Meghan's phone rang again, she looked at the caller ID: Agent Smith FBI. She looked to Jan, "Should we record it this time?" Jan shook her head, "No need. She's right. You need an incident to use anything she says."

Meghan answered, "Hi… is there more?"

“More? More what, Ms. Woods?”

Meghan went cold ~ it wasn’t dot’s voice. “Agent Smith?”

“Yes, ma’am. I’m calling about this morning.”

“This morning?”

“Yes, ma’am. If the suspect tries to reach out to you, please call me immediately.”

“Agent Smith, you seem to keep trying to step around the Constitution of the United States of America.”

“No ma’am. I’m trying to protect you. Your life is in grave danger. If you are ever near the suspect, well, we’d hate for there to be any chance of collateral damage.”

“Is that what the kids are calling it these days, Agent Smith?”

“Kids, ma’am?”

“It’s a euphemism, Agent Smith. If I was your copyeditor I would encourage you to refrain from using words that could be construed as threatening.”

“Noted, ma’am. If you are refusing a protection detail, I can only offer best practices and guidelines for your safety, ma’am. In addition, I would like to discuss exchanging resources to support both our objectives.”

“Our?”

"Yes, ma'am. The Objectives of protecting and serving the citizens of the United States of America. I trust that's your motivation as well. I'm offering to support you with information in exchange for you supporting us with yours."

"Well, Agent Smith, seeing as how I broke open your case yesterday, it seems the ledger on your side is dry."

"The person representing themself as a department of corrections Officer Taylor was… not ever credentialed as such. We believe she was working in association with the suspect, State Inmate number W10042574."

"Not news, Agent Smith. We uncovered that yesterday with a simple Google search. Also, you need a new working name for State Inmate number W10042574, it's never gonna fly over a radio."

"Noted ma'am. The person representing themself as Officer Taylor is about to be arrested and taken into Federal Custody."

Meghan stood and looked at her phone, then set it on Jan's desk, remembering dot's lesson from earlier, "Where?"

"Not at liberty to disclose ma'am, you, of course, understand. But she will be brought to the FBI Field Office in Jolliet. I can arrange an interview after her booking.

"Before she's assigned or arranges for an attorney? Agent Smith, that's a big offer."

"It's all I got for now. Ledger balanced?"

"We'll see."

The call ended. Meghan looked to Jan, "This is getting…"

"Interesting."

"I was going to say, spooky. But you'd redline the fuck out of that."

"You're right. But you've always been using a different style guide."

11

"

Any day that starts with a little bump and ends with Narcan is never a good day…

"

Things were certainly easier, thought Meghan as she jumped from the car hired for her by Asphere. She could get used to rockstar status as Lucas called it. The car would be waiting for her and anywhere else she needed to be to keep the story going.

"Keep the story going," Jan's words were ringing in her ears as she walked up the steps to Western Illinois Field Office. She flinched when Jan first said them as they stood before the VP of accounting, as Jan informed the VP that Meghan was probably not in a position to be spending her time getting herself from point A to point B, and keeping track of receipts, so a company credit card and an expense account were long overdue, you know, to keep the story going."

But, here Meghan was about to open the door to the FBI Field Office and the next stage of her career…

Inside she found several other media professionals. She recognized reporters from the AP, Al Jeezera, and Fox. A host of others were obvious by their tailored suits and coiffed hair. She took a breath and looked for a place to… be.

Agent Smith saw her before she saw him. They nodded subtle acknowledgment to each other. Meghan wondered if these people had also been promised interviews.

Outside, a black SUV slowed to a stop, then continued around the building to the back entrance. Meghan guessed that someone had alerted them of the full lobby of thirsty press, but the fact was, they would never bring a suspect through the front public-facing door.

It would be another forty minutes before the pool feed monitors showed the booking process, which, though similar to a local police precincts' methods were more a show for the press than practical. The FBI already had a suspect on file and in their database before any arrest, and this was also a way to remove temptations and allegations of potential abuse, not unlike the pre-inspection one does when renting a car, circling any dents that were there before taking ownership.

This time Meghan saw it right away. If she'd learned nothing else in the last few weeks it was that she needed to always be observant. Whoever this person was, she wasn't Officer Taylor or the woman whom she'd known as Officer Taylor, anyway.

But this time, rather than throwing her pearls before anyone, she'd keep her observation to herself. The mug shot was projected onto the video screens around the complex.

When the FBI incident commander stepped into the official Press briefing room, Meghan had been seated in the front row. She couldn't decide if this was to butter her up or keep her close. Either way, Meghan tried to formulate a question that wouldn't tip her hand and was surprised that right after the official statement of, "The person of interest who had been impersonating an Illinois Department of Corrections Officer has been brought into custody, apprehended in the Emergency Room of Jolliet General Hospital," Meghan was the first recognized to ask a follow-up question.

"Thank you. Meghan Woods from Asphere. Had the injuries, specifically the bruising around the eyes and nose of your suspect been addressed at Jolliet General ER, or were they treated here at your field office?"

The IC looked to his staff for answers but blank stares and questioning shakes of heads was his reply. He looked to Meghan, "I'm… going to have to get back to you about that?"

"Asking a Follow-up, was the Incident Commander supervising just the FBI, or were you in charge of an interagency effort?"

The IC's eyes narrowed as they ducked from Meghan's shade, staring at her with thinly veiled contempt at her calling out his ignorance. He started to speak. Smiled. Started again, then nodded at her like a fencer who'd just been tagged under his mask. "This was an interagency operation, and we are grateful for the IBI, Illinois state police, and the officers out at Stateville. It was a total team effort."

Agent Smith took the empty seat next to Meghan while the IC moved on to other questions of which Meghan could care less. "So… I take it the follow-up is no longer necessary?"

Meghan turned to Agent Smith, "On the contrary. I love a good comedy show. And just so we're clear, the ledger still needs balancing. That's two for me, zilch for you."

Agent Smith was waiting for Meghan in the hallway after the Briefing ended. The IC locked eyes with her as he turned to leave, but she pretended to be more interested in Agent Smith. "We never saw her face. She must've been hiding under the bed when we escorted the person we thought was W100-42-574."

Meghan shook her head, "Still workshopping, I see. Needs more work. And…?"

"And, so… how severe was the bruising?"

"And here I thought that while you were away you were actually looking back at the surveillance video to check my facts."

"They… were… erased."

Meghan laughed out loud. She covered her mouth as everyone turned to look at her, she didn't even feign apology. "She is fucking playing you all like a goddamned Stradivarius. Maybe that's what you should be calling her. Her eyes looked like she was peeking out from two blood oranges! You could barely see her… eyes. But… of course. She…"

"She what?"

Meghan looked around, the other crews were packing up, having gotten what they came for, they were off to other stories, "She… is better at this than you. The only hope you have is if she ever decides to turn herself in again."

"We have this suspect. We can turn her."

"I wouldn't bet on that. I'm sure whoever you think you have is so not anything, that you'll be forced to retract all of this and set them free without so much as a bad lead to waste your chasing. But that's just a guess."

"So, you don't even want to talk to her?"

Meghan looked at Agent Smith, "You sure you want me doing your work for you? You can't help but use me, can you?"

Agent Smith's shoulder shrugged, "It would help me a lot. I wouldn't have to charge them or wait for them to lawyer up and I could get them out of her on the way back home before this completely blows up in our face."

Meghan shrugged. "This will cost you severely, but sure. I'm as patriotic as the next girl."

Even though she was helping the FBI, it still creeped Meghan out to hear the door slam behind her. The woman sitting at the cold steel table was nothing at all like Officer Taylor. dot was right, they had continually underestimated her to their utter peril, from jump.

"They told you I was a reporter and that nothing in here is protected?" The woman nodded without looking up. "So, I'm not here for anything other than making sure you get out of here as quickly as possible. Can I call you…?"

"Taylor."

"Nice. Okay, Taylor. How did you get here… why did they arrest you?"

"I had been in the emergency room. I… OD'd."

"Fucking hell." Meghan looked to the large two-way mirror and bit her lip, "I don't… you idiots." She sat down and looked at Taylor, "Are you okay?"

"Any day that starts with a little bump and ends with Narcan is never a good day."

"Did they tell you anything about what's going on?"

"They said I helped someone escape from prison. I told them I hadn't been back in 18 months. "

Meghan stood up. She squeezed Taylor's shoulder, "I'm sorry these morons can't seem to find their ass with both hands, I hope you get home soon." Meghan walked to the door and waited for the electronic bolt to open and she stepped out almost slamming into Agent Smith's chest.

"Shit" She pulled up in time. "Ms. Woods, you don't have to be so disrespectful."

"Respect is something earned, Agent Smith. This is fucking embarrassing. Get that woman on her way as we agreed, please. I've got so many other things to do."

Agent Smith rubbed his eyes, "We got a tip that Taylor was in an Emergency room, having been brought in by ambulance, and…"

"Who the fuck are you guys?

You're supposed to be the F- Fucking B-I? Protecting our country from… what? Junkies? That clown you call an Incident Commander didn't even know how bad you all had fucked up? Who does that?"

Agent Smith dropped all professional pretense, "Ms. Woods. I know you have many biases against us…"

Meghan's eyes narrowed like a cobra, she hissed, "Agent Smith, I sincerely hope you are not about to question my patriotism or my professionalism…"

Agent Smith pulled up, "I'm sorry, I meant no… the truth is, we got nothing."

Meghan shook her head, "I. Am. Out. Of. Words. Goodbye, Agent Smith."

It sounded like machine gun fire. The hired car hadn't even pulled away from the curb before Meghan was already typing away on her laptop. She had an organic in to information that dot had given her earlier today, as well as a way to show how badly everyone had botched this case via the press briefing. None of the other bureaus understood the shade she threw at the IC, believing that the suspect was who they said she was.

She was going to scoop them all.

12

"

These are second date questions, or if you're really cute,

3rd martini at the very least…

"

When her phone rang and Agent Smith's caller ID came up, she considered letting it go to voicemail but remembered it could be a spoof.

Which it was, "Hello Meghan. You'll be happy to know that Taylor two is on her way home."

"Poor girl. But what did happen to Officer Taylor? And who were those people in the body bags?"

"That's two short questions with two very long answers. Officer Taylor is very long gone. I'm sad, she's really good at this. But, one and done is the rule. She's safe and on the other side of the world in her dream life. The corpses in those body bags were Johns and a Jane Doe that had come from a morgue in Iowa, on their way to a medical school in Jolliet."

"You don't even have a tattoo do you?"

"I beg your pardon. Those are second-date questions. Or, if you're really cute, third martini at the very least."

"How did you survive that crash?"

"Crash?"

"Yes, the two cars that the guards were chasing you with. All three cars were burning. They said the rotorwash…"

"Was used to get the Marshalls to stop."

Meghan held her breath, "Yeah… fucking hell. That was you?"

"My other car is a helicopter."

"Okay, hold on, how?"

"Look, I told you a long time ago, Boys like to follow orders. So, the trick is to be the one giving them. They all wear headsets and listen for their name to be called and a task given to them. They never think to question them. No one wondered why their commander had them circle the Pen a number of times to secure the perimeter before joining the chase. No one wondered how the wreckage got where it was, they just all arrived to find burning cars. And no one thought for a moment to question the Prison guards until they were all… gone."

"Giving everyone plenty of time to vanish forever," said Meghan shaking her head.

"And by the time they realized they should've looked closer for real evidence and leads, it was irrelevant. Who they were looking for was never there in the first place."

"But that would take a huge team of help… drivers, cars, explosions… you said you only act alone."

"I say a lot of things."

"So you do have help."

"Not totally sure what we're talking about."

The call ended and Meghan felt some kind of way. About life. About The FBI. About the baby Trans growing up in this world.

She still felt that way as she entered Jan's office. Jan looked up from the article she'd sent from the car, "It's almost 180 from what the AP has already posted, were they even at the same briefing?" Meghan slung her backpack over the armrest of the couch and collapsed into it, "dot called it, they'll probably announce tomorrow that they had the wrong person and then the retractions and firings will begin."

Jan sat up, "Well, then we have to post tonight. We still need another five thousand words if we're going to push the cover story off. Come on Wunderkind, tempus fugit."

Meghan sat up, "Well, I'll get a jump on it to make the line, but… dot told me to watch my scanner tonight."

"Oh my. One last hurrah? A swan song?"

Meghan shrugged.

Lucas called to see if Meghan needed dinner, "It's been a while since you pulled ambulance detail."

"Thanks, babe but Jan ordered us delivery. I'll keep you posted, miss you!"

They both kept one eye on the scanner as Meghan wrote and Jan edited and added links. They had a scathing post without any added fireworks but were prepared to scrap the ending for any revelations or events that came from whatever dot had in store for the evening.

The scanner had the usual Saturday night traffic, which in Chicago like all other Metro areas would be rife with more gun violence than any third-world war zone. It wasn't until they heard that an Incident Command task force was rolling toward downtown that their blood ran cold, despite anticipating it all day.

At first, Meghan & Jan just stared at each other, unsure how to respond, then they both snapped out of the spell at once, grabbing jackets and backpacks, they headed for the garage. Jan called their in-house security team as the elevator closed and soon they all met in one of Asphere's black Suburbans. The radio traffic was frantic and soon would be jammed, but a battalion of first responders was heading for Daley Plaza and the firecrews and bombsquad would, it seemed, get there first.

13

"

We can't be seen throwing the FBI under the bus. They do a good job of that by themselves -- they don't need our help.

"

The driver dropped Meghan, Jan, and their security team off and they joined a growing crowd that was being held back by hastily assembled barricades. Meghan tried pushing her way into the crowd but was never going to make it, until one of her security team, a large man who introduced himself as Orlando put his hulking arm around Meghan's waist and plowed through the crowd with gentle authority, practically carrying her like a football. He was deft and effective, people naturally flowed to one side or another of his outstretched hamhock of a hand like water on the prow of a destroyer.

And just like that, Meghan found herself as far as the police would allow, the only thing between the plaza and her was the thin yellow plastic tape. With Orlando behind her, she had an unobstructed view of…

Three gagged men. White zip ties handcuffing their hands to overly large bibles, they stood a socially distant six feet or so from each other, a red braided rope binding their arms to their sides at the elbows and to each other, like climbers on a glacier, or inmates on a chain gang.

A sign warning all to stay back 25 feet, *"lest the chemicals that soaked each bible mix to produce a fiery death,"* was underlined by a line connecting three black dots. The men were clearly freaked out, sweating despite the spring chill, ties, and collars loosed.

The News media was racing to set up; the bombsquad too, hurrying to get an officer's protective suit on, ambulances at the ready. Everyone seemed to be waiting for a signal or sign of some sort. The gagged man in the center of the chain, wet his pants in fear.

Meghan was looking back to find where Jan had gotten when she heard it: A faint whistling, as if something was coming from above. She looked up to see a glowing light flying… or… *falling* toward them…

It hit the ground at the feet of the man in the center, smashing into a cloud of glass and fire, igniting his pants which in turn ignited his bible and the rope connecting him to his two companions. Fire shot down both ropes like a fuse setting their bibles aflame, exposing a steel cable that kept them tethered at the waist despite the heat. Each man stared in horror as their handcuffed hands were unable to let go of the bibles even as their skin was set ablaze.

All three men were quickly engulfed in fire. PANIC ripped through the crowd as everyone ran for cover. Orlando pulled Meghan into his embrace as he used his back to shield her from the bodies darting in fear and adrenaline. He saw a clear path and carried her through to the waiting Suburban that drove up onto the curb. Jan and her security guard were in the back seat a step ahead of them, and soon all were fleeing through the streets as other first responders were rushing toward the mayhem. Meghan turned to see a firetruck's water cannon hit one of the burning men in the chest so hard it cut the body in half, leaving only the torso still connected to the other burning corpses.

"Stop!" shouted Meghan, "We have to be here." The driver looked to Jan and she nodded, "Let's let it die down and then we'll need to talk to the first responders." The driver pulled to the side and up onto a sidewalk vantage point. From up here, she could see the point of dot's mayhem. As the three burning hulks collapsed into piles of charred bone and ash, they were reduced to…

… three dots connected by the single line created by the cable. Meghan used her iPhone to snap a pic.

It had taken another hour of chaos before any of the Incident Command's office would entertain their request for an interview. Even dropping Agent Smith's name had been no use. Finally, the Chicago Fire's spokesperson declined all attempts at identifying the victims or the suspect or any motive, confining their responses to the things a fire department would be concerned with, namely the department's response: three companies, the use of a chemical accelerant combined with an ignition chemical and the department's policy of withholding speculation pending the forensic lab's analysis.

"All of which would've been hard to deny with so many eyewitnesses," agreed Meghan, as they walked back to the Suburban, under the watchful eye of Orlando, "but seriously, I don't know why they even bothered."

"They got nothing," quipped Jan as Orlando opened the door for her, "They're all…"

Meghan slid in beside her, "Circling the wagons… they know they don't know... shit."

They continued to work from the back seat of the Suburban while Orlando and the security team kept a watchful eye. Meghan could tell they were not happy about being a mobile unit and despite the last of the responders still cordoning off the Plaza, it was trying to settle back into its default setting of the occasional oblivious Downtown barhoppers and diners mingling with scattered nighttime unhoused people.

Jan was insistent that they get a better response from anyone in the Incident Command team and they teased that the Mayor's office had agreed to send a response team for a press conference.

Meghan watched as the news had obviously been spread because the other press teams were all staring at their phones simultaneously and settling back into a "hurry and wait" stance.

Cameras were trained on the Plaza, but their operators were chatting with their engineers, Reporters compared notes with Producers.

Meghan's iPhone shot of the dots of ash staining the sidewalk of Daley Plaza would haunt everyone. The Asphere photo editor, a seasoned old bear of a man named Roger, remarked as they spoke over Jan's speakerphone that it "smelled of Pulitzer worthiness." Meghan and Jan rolled their eyes, and said in stereo, "If only you could smell it from our end." A sob caught in Meghan's throat, "I don't think I'll ever get the smell of burning human out of my nostrils." Her rush of emotion caught Jan off guard, but she put her arm around the younger reporter with unspoken compassion.

Roger must've sensed by the silence that Meghan had just crossed a professional Rubicon, because he didn't respond for some time, giving Meghan a chance to process, when he finally spoke, he thanked Meghan for making his job easy, and sent another photo, saying, "Can you confirm this caption for accuracy?" The photo was one that Meghan wasn't sure was useful, but the Editor had blown up and enhanced the image of the burned note paper that had hung around the neck of the State Senator. Only the connected dots were readable with the exception of the words: "*lest the bible*" and *"fiery."* Under the photo, the Editor had captioned it with, "The FBI has been reluctant to disclose the killer's calling card, connecting this murder to 47 confessed kills."

Jan raised an eyebrow, "Um… We can't be seen throwing the FBI under the bus. They do a pretty good job of that by themselves, they don't need our help."

"I think the picture speaks for itself," said Meghan, "does it need a caption other than a locator?"

Roger agreed that it did not.

Jan nodded, "Hit send, my friend."

Roger laughed, "Done. It's in the web team's hands now."

14

“

Spoof positive.

”

Meghan’s story would also be the one that broke who the victims were. It had been a text from Agent Smith. It took Meghan connecting the names with the links provided to realize they were, “spoof positive.”

“What? asked Jan as she looked at Meghan, “Please don’t tell me…”

“dot spoofed Agent Smith’s phone again.”

“Well, okay, but…” Jan slid over to look at Meghan’s phone as she followed the link to a video recording on YouTube. They saw a video of three men with Bibles handcuffed to their wrists standing in a darkened room, their faces lit by a single bulb. They heard a familiar voice say "Say your names and occupations please."

The men were sweaty, scared, defiance had already left them. The first man declared himself as "Dr. Kevin Roberts, The CEO of The Heritage Foundation." The Second man was "Jonathan Reid, Lobbyist for the Christian Front." And the Third, the man in the center, "Illinois State Senator Neil Anderson, and let me tell you, you will be prosecuted to the fullest…"

The video was flooded with light as a door behind them opened and they were told, "Walk out to the square, if you hope to get out of this alive. Chicago's Finest might be able to help you. Oh and make sure you stay 6 feet apart, or those chemicals in your good books will mix and you will be turned into human Birthday candles."

The camera showed them walking out into Daley Plaza, as a crowd was beginning to gather. The voice was right, Firefighters were waiting for them, but when they smelled the chemicals they were ordered to "STOP RIGHT THERE." The video cut off abruptly.

"Oof, Meghan, this… this will never clear legal without a fight," said Jan, but Meghan was already digging into the web, finding the state senator's infamous speech calling for violence during a floor debate in the Illinois Senate about gender-neutral bathrooms, *"I'm telling you right now, if a guy walks in there, I'm going to beat the living piss out of him,"* as his supporters cheered. *"So, this is going to cause violence, and it's going to cause violence from dads like me."*

Meghan turned her computer for Jan to see, who didn't waste a moment, digging into her computer for campaign contributions and discovering, that Dr. Kevin, the newly minted CEO of the right-wing nonprofit "think tank," The Heritage Foundation had been the largest donor to Senator Anderson's campaign.

It didn't take Jan more than a minute to find that Mr. Reid had been employed by not only the The Legacy Foundation, but also The Christian Crusades, and Family Focus First, "Aren't all three of those listed as Hate Groups by the Southern Poverty Law Center?"

Meghan saw her laptop was running out of juice, "This seems to be a different page of dot's playbook… she's… abandoned all pretense. Orlando, would you have a way for me to plug in?" Orlando grinned and reached back for her cord, she handed it to him as he nodded to the driver who turned the ignition on. Orlando opened the glove box and a custom panel of every imaginable AC & DC connector available. He plugged her in, then went back to surveilling their surroundings.

Jan shook her head, "She's more than sending a message. She's taunting them, she's poking the FBI in the…eye. To what end?"

Meghan resumed typing on her computer, "Can we recall the post? She's flagrantly saying, you haven't seen us? You erasing us? Then you will never see us coming."

"Meghan… we can't scoop the FBI. They haven't had the time to even notify the next of kin. This is one Lily that doesn't need any gilding."

"Jan, we both know that their names have already leaked. It was on YouTube. You connected the dots in less than 30 seconds."

Jan rubbed her eyes, "I can let 'em know we're sending them an addendum. Get on it."

Meghan's fingers were already flying.

Orlando came back to the Suburban with three large pizzas, the famed Chicago style which was only called "Deep dish" outside Illinois was just referred to as pie, had certainly grown up. Surprisingly, Orlando didn't need special instructions from Meghan as he himself was not only a vegan, but also a competitive bodybuilder, who was known on Instagram as Plant Power

Perfection, so he and Meghan shared a pie while the security team and Jan happily devoured the pepperoni & onion.

They had finished the pizza when the commotion in the Plaza suddenly started. A woman in a suit rolled out a podium and took two portable teleprompter mirrors on lightweight stands and set them up near the crime scene. The camera crews all rushed to move their cameras and reporters to the new area jockeying for the best positions as Meghan's phone rang, she showed Jan the caller ID: Agent Smith, as she hit answer and speaker. "Hello Meghan," said dot with a weird feedback quality to the sound, "you've been a busy bee during all this drama."

Meghan looked around. "You've got a good ear," said dot, "I'm to your right." Meghan looked across the Plaza to the steps that led up to the Citibank building and saw a figure waving at her from the pillars, "and a good eye."

"Hi, dot. Isn't this a little dangerous? I mean…"

"Oh, honey, aren't you sweet. I just took a moment to let you know that there's no need to waste your time with this press conference. It will just be a repeat of the Fire Department Spokesperson's vagueness. An attempt of calming fears by appearing to be in control of the situation."

"We figured, but Jan's wanting a little more of the official response to balance out our reporting."

"No shade to Jan," they could see dot waving again, "Hi Jan, but the ol' false equivalency is so… pre Fox-Dominion, ain't it?"

Jan waved as she leaned into the phone, "It's still a point of our journalistic style sheet, thank you all the same."

"You do you, Jan."

"So… dot…"

"Yes, Meghan?"

"Was that the only reason you called?"

"No. I called to say goodbye. One thing I can't be risking is your life. Once Agent Smith gets wise that he's been being used, he'll have nowhere to go but to harass you. Besides, you don't need me to do your job."

"Well thank you, but… this last one was outside your normal M-O as the police would say. Is this your solution to the mission?"

Jan was typing as Meghan held the phone, "Solution? I'm still not sold on it myself. I need to have a think on it and we'll see what the rest of the world does with this one and what *dots they connect.*"

"It sounds like you like that name."

"I told you, it was growing on me."

"Yes, but what if they don't connect them back to you? To your mission, your purpose? What's going to be the point, your point, of all this… death?"

"I suppose that's for them to decide."

"dot, that's not like you to give them the power to control the narrative."

"That's why I'm so fond of you Meghan, dear. You have such a way with words."

Meghan watched as dot waved and made a large point of reluctantly ending the call on her cell phone, throwing the phone into a trashcan, and slipping into the crowd.

Meghan and Jan tried to follow her as she stepped down into the throng when suddenly the trashcan EXPLODED and shattered the glass of the entrance to the building. The crowd PANICKED and darted in several directions for cover, two Officers of the Mayor's Security detail tackled the Mayor and covered her with their bodies as other Officers stood in a perimeter with guns drawn.

Fuck, dot…" whispered Meghan as she quickly scanned the chaos,

"That bitch is… gone."

ABOUT THE AUTHOR

Mara Anne McQuire is the oldest of five girls, but by no means the most mature. Content to be the crazy aunt who has no idea how to change a diaper or her mind, Ms. McQuire can be found curled up with Belladonna, her weim/pitt cross, a cookbook and a glass of something red. She collects cookbooks, spatulas and whisks, and never met a fight she didn't like.

www.ingramcontent.com/pod-product-compliance
Lightning Source LLC
LaVergne TN
LVHW020719110826
845149LV00012B/2333

* 9 7 9 8 9 9 5 8 9 8 8 0 1 *